Of Rhetoric and Redemption in La Rioja

JIM TALLMON

RESOURCE *Publications* · Eugene, Oregon

OF RHETORIC AND REDEMPTION IN LA RIOJA

Resource Publications
An Imprint of Wipf and Stock Publishers
199 W. 8th Ave., Suite 3
Eugene, OR 97401

www.wipfandstock.com

PAPERBACK ISBN: 978-1-4982-9396-9
HARDCOVER ISBN: 978-1-4982-9398-3
EBOOK ISBN: 978-1-4982-9397-6

Manufactured in the U.S.A.   MAY 24, 2017

Of Rhetoric and Redemption in La Rioja

Contents

Acknowledgments | *vii*

1   Prelude | 1

2   Farewell to our Brother and Friend | 7

3   Off to Spain | 11

4   Three Days in Ostia | 15

5   Paul Seeks Wise Counsel | 27

6   Formulating a "Battle Plan" | 33

7   In Tarraco | 40

8   Paul and Quintilian Meet | 49

9   Clement Catches Up | 66

10   Wisdom and Eloquence | 70

11   The Grand Tour | 83

12   Rhetoric: The Intellectual Love of God | 102

13   To the Far Shore and Back Again | 118

14   Harvest Time in Caesaraugusta | 123

15   End Game | 131

16   *Metanoia* | 136

Glossary | *141*
Index | *143*

Acknowledgments

THE WORK OF GEORGE Alexander Kennedy has both inspired and instructed me over the years, both when it comes to Quintilian and, especially, with regard to rhetorical theory. So I wish to acknowledge Professor Kennedy's contribution to this novel, even though I never got the chance to discuss it with him, face to face, as I had hoped. I hope it somehow merits his admiration. Much of the dialogue was shaped by what I learned of Richard M. Weaver's view of the relationship of rhetoric to dialectic from my mentor, Dr. Charles Follette. He has had a significant impact on me, both intellectually and spiritually, since the 1980's. I wish to acknowledge the support of my wife, Bonnie, my daughter, her husband, and their babies. Thank you for providing a space in which I could, at long last, spend some time writing this story, after more than a decade of "thinking it through." I hope this story not only introduces my grandchildren to The Good, but guides them to the Giver of all good gifts. Thank you to my friend, Dr. Christian Kopff, who offered assistance with a thorny Latin question. I wish to acknowledge Mr. Zach Beck for your help with research. Your eager contributions were most welcome and always substantive. Also, to the students of Patrick Henry College who helped with that initial background research. And my friend Vicki Michaels. Thanks for explaining the finer points of weaving! Your early interest in the storyline encouraged me. Thank you, all. I hope you enjoy this little book. It would not have been possible without you. Finally, to the good people at Wipf and Stock, thanks for your assistance, for wise counsel, and for your hard work.

1

Prelude

SLOWLY, IMPERCEPTIBLY, HIS HEAD swayed from side to side, coming to rest in his crepey yet uncalloused hands. He lay there, motionless, straining to form a meaningful thought. But could manage only questions. He was so filled with self-doubt, so utterly exhausted, his faculties were crippled. "Why the sacrifice? Why so very much effort? So much sweat? What could I possibly gain by writing this overwrought, redundant, and massive treatise? How could I add anything meaningful to the study of rhetoric that hasn't already been said? It's all been said. You are not up to the task. The bit about pedagogy may be of some interest, I suppose, but it is so pedantic!"

"Beg your pardon, Sir. May I . . . " "Oh!" startled, he jumped. "Yes. Yes, of course. Water. . . . No. Make it wine. Last year's Burdigalian blend" he hoped the wine would restore some semblance of coherence, or, at least, stifle the questions. "Very well, Sir."

Head in hands, elbows planted on his desk, he stared long and hard at the manuscript before him. It was tear-stained, again. "Drat," he scolded himself. "Am I unhinged? I don't rightly know, but at least my self-loathing is focused! Heh, heh."

"Oh, Veronica!" He gazed upon her, in his mind's eye, gently rocking little Quintilian; his "Little Angel," flowers in her long, brown hair; large, round, dark eyes that always gave him pause. "Soooo beautiful! Cruel Fates, why have you done this? Oh, my boys . . . " he wailed aloud. Moaning, the tears came flooding as he shoved to the side his manuscript, sparing it another drenching. "I need you." Silence. Despair. A knock at the door. "Your wine, Sir." Master was a pitiful sight. Inconsolable; lost in work. The master gestured in the direction of the corner of his writing table, without looking up. He didn't like being seen in this condition. As soon as the servant re-treated, the sobs returned. Wave after wave after wave. . . .

Now the room is dark. Without lifting his head or clearing his mind, he opened a single eye to glance at the waning moon. Morning would come in an hour or two. Knowing approximately what time it is has no effect on his being. He is not curious. He is no longer in the throes of overweening grief. He is no longer overcome with self-doubt about a writing project that had consumed him for more than two years now. He just . . . is. He sips his wine but does not taste it.

"Veronicahaaach," he yelled her name, blubbering, choking on her name. "Oh, Pieeeetras! M-m-m-my little Quintilian! why did I not take more care for your souls?"! "Forgivvvvve me." I was so focused on myself. So consumed with ambition, he thought. And political pressures . . . "Idiot! You were warned. 'Time is short,' Clemens said. 'We know not the hour,' he said. I scoffed. And, why shouldn't I have scoffed. It is rot!" Grief gave way to rage. He backhanded the goblet onto the floor. "It's *nonesense*," he screamed, his voice cracking under the strain. I serve the Dieties of my fatherland! What hath a man of my stature to do with these foreign gods? With this Jesus of Nazareth?! Vanity. I am vain. Veronica was right. My vanity cost me my happiness, my love and my children."

"Where is that confounded cleaning rag," he got up from the table, looking aimlessly, unable to gather his wits even enough to clean up after his ridiculous outburst. He hoisted the lamp and shuffled to the corner. No rag. Perhaps it's in this clay jar. He removes the lid and finds, not a rag, but a familiar, prized scroll. "Ah. Haven't seen this in years. Paul's letter to the Roman Christians." He stroked it once, slowly, fondly, eyes closed, replaced it, and took up the rag he'd found next to the clay pot and absent-mindedly sopped up the wine that stained the tile floor. But the touch, that single touch, let loose a torrent of memories.

He was transported. "Mmmmm. Ahhh . . . yessss" nodding as he sopped, without purpose. He was elsewhere. "No. It had to be early 68! Wait. Did I just utilize Christian dating conventions?" Here came a slow, agonized sigh. "He was dead by the end of that . . . damned Nero." He remi-nisced further, this time savoring the splash of superb Burdigalian Red that had not ended up on the floor. Guests had commented, more than once, how much they enjoyed this blend!

"It was only yesterday . . . We were on the veranda." He remembered a beautiful sunset, framed between snow-capped peaks and heaven above, mirrored in the River Iberus, as it skirted the estate, at the base of verdant, boulder-strewn, hills, just beyond his beloved olive grove. He had spent many a happy hour playing Centurion amongst those trees. "I think he sought me out in the Provincial Forum. Yes. I invited him to sup. Through the mists of time he is little more than an apparition. We had a brief week together, back in those halcyon days in The Tarraconensis, about the time Galba took me with him to Rome . . . what a mess that turned out to be! Never should have left the home place." He laid his head, or face rather, flat on the desk, not bothering to cushion it with folded hands, and took several breaths. He could bear no more unpleasantness; even so remote an unpleasantness. Somehow, the rhythm of his breath settled his troubled mind, so that floodgates opened, and relentless questions were replaced with pleasant memories.

"Yes, a good man; intelligent, too. I remember him often. Damned Nero." Although he was behind a closed door, in the middle of the night, his (admittedly dangerous) thoughts unnerved him. His head bolted upright; he looked around, reflexively; bit his tongue.

"It was after a day before the praetor, in Caesaraugus . . . no. *Tarraco*." The memories helped restore coherence. "In Tarraco. Yes. Regarding the matter of, of Apro-uh, Apronianus."

⌁

" . . . Sabinus?" Marcus Fabius Quintilianus, the up-and-coming young patron of the Provincial Courts in Tarraco had to ask a second time: "Did you not understand me the first time? 'At the time you say you witnessed Naevius Apronianus throw his wife from the tower, did you have an unobstructed view of the window from which he threw her'?"

"No."

"No, what?"

"No, my view was obstructed by the rooftops of the buildings between me and their home. I did not see the window. I saw her hit the street. I saw her head . . . I saw her—"

"*Then* what did you do?"

"I, I do not remember. I was scared. It is misty in my head. I, I hid my eyes."

"Sabinus. It is important that you make yourself remember."

3

"I hid my eyes because I could not believe what I had just seen. I wished I could unsee it. She looked horrible, with the blood and the skull wide open . . . and . . ."

"That will be quite enough, Sabinus. What did you do *next*?"

"I yelled for help, then I ran out to the street."

"Out of which window were you looking when you saw the unfortunate woman fall to the street?"

"My shop window, on the second floor, above the entry."

"And how many steps are there down to street level from your shop?"

"Um, one, two . . ."

Sabinus closed his eyes and counted the steps out as he pictured himself bounding down them to street level. "Ten."

"With a landing as well, I presume?"

"Yes. With a landing as well."

"And how far from your front door to the scene of this unfortunate circumstance?"

"About, I don't know, fifteen paces."

"Sorry, Sabinus. I need you to be very precise."

"Fifteen, yes, fifteen paces."

"Walking or running, that is, a longer stride?"

"Yes, fifteen long strides."

"So, from the time you saw the wife of Naevius Apronianus hit the ground to the time you arrived by her side on the street was, maybe 30 seconds?"

"No. Longer. Nearly a full minute. I froze. I did not know if I should, should go down there. . . ."

"Okay, thank you. So, nearly a minute later, after you had screamed, had faltered, then run downstairs and out to the scene, whom did you find there?"

"Nobody."

"Nobody? Really? How can this be? You have nobody else to testify to the veracity of your account?"

"The street was empty. When I looked up, Señor Apronianus was standing in the window. And he looked strange."

"Wait. We'll get to the look on his face in a moment. Where were the neighbors?"

"Out for the day, I suppose. It was Saturn's Day, and very sunny and bright. Early."

"Early, eh? How early?"

"The sun had been up about an hour and one half."

"So, you are telling this court that you saw Señor Apronianus push his wife from the window."

"Yes. I saw him push his wife from the window, and when I saw him standing there, he looked very guilty to me."

"Did you, and this is very important, Sabinus, justice is our aim here, did you see the accused, Naevius, push his wife with his own hands from that window?"

"No. But he did it."

"Thank you. You admit, now, under cross-examination, that you did not actually see him push her out the window. You say he looked strange?"

"Yes. He had this look in his eye. The eyes of a madman."

"'The eyes of a madman,' you say? So, you saw the victim hit the ground; you froze for a minute, then ran to the street, looked up and saw Naevius Apronianus standing there with 'the look of a madman.' Could you please describe that look?"

"No, not really. I do not have the words."

"Please try."

"Well . . . " Quintilian leaned against the edge of the half wall that separated the jury from the patricians. A peculiar gentleman, back in the shadows, seated between the patricians and his own clerk, caught his eye. "Yes, do elaborate for the court." Sabinus was still talking, but saying absolutely nothing.

He made a very poor first impression. But, still, there was something about him; a glint of intelligence beneath the grubby exterior. Even through the mists of time the image of that shabby looking man . . . Quintilian sat very still, at the table in his writer's garret, barely breathing, so as not to disturb the image. Whether it was the wine or simply a need for clarity, focus returned; the apparition taking on flesh and bone. "I was drawn to him," he recalled, mumbling to no one in particular. "He certainly looked silly there, next to the patricians, in his traveling tunic and filthy cape." Ha! A more Hebrew looking gentleman, he thought, I cannot imagine! Still, there was an air of intelligence, a worldliness, about him that piqued my interest. Something in the eye.

"I'm glad," shaking his head very slightly, "I invited him to accompany me to . . . to . . . " His index finger held from pursed lips to the tip of his nose, then dancing across the space in front of his eyes, pointing to a map forming in his fancy. "I was pleading the case in Tarraco; had to spend the week at the villa; loose ends to tie-off before I set out for Rome. Yes, it was the villa. We met in Caesaraugusta then rode together to the plantation. I do not believe I've had a more stimulating conversation all the years, since. Then, it was off to Rome. "Nero!" he exclaimed aloud, quite forgetting himself, spitting on the floor in disgust. "Had his head in a fortnight! But he got his. . . . not a week later."

2

Farewell to our Brother and Friend

(EARLY JUNE 68 A.D., TWO MILES OUT OF ROME, NEAR THE PORT OF OSTIA)

THE CORPSE WAS LAID to rest in a tomb beside a meadow surrounded by oaks, past an olive grove, not far from the northeastern boundary of Lucina's estate.[1] Barbarians! Wouldn't release the head. Said Nero had "other plans for that." One can only imagine.

I thanked those assembled and began: "The last time we gathered here and enjoyed Lucina's hospitality, only a short season ago, was a happy occasion. We were preparing to embark on one final missionary adventure with our brother and friend, whom today, with heavy hearts, we lay to rest in this meadow, sheltered by the canopy of these mighty oaks."

"Thank you, again, Lucina," turning, palm upturned, and smiling at her, "for your hospitality." Turning back to the throng that filled the meadow, "Only forty some days ago you bid a joyous farewell to Brother Paul, as together our company set out, in fulfillment of Christ's great testament, and in fulfillment of Brother Paul's great desire to bring the Gospel of the Lord to the Western shores of the world. But now, alone, he crosses to that Heavenly Shore, where he may finally rest from his labors. And we bid him a tearful, 'Farewell.'"

"Our blessed brother and father is no more. But he has gone to a better place. He has gone on to his heavenly reward; he is 'poured out as a drink

---

1. According to church lore, Paul's remains were laid to rest on the estate of Lucina, a woman of the faith who lived near the second mile marker outside Rome on the way to Ostia.

offering.' But, my friends, have we *truly* lost him? No. He is still with us, for it was his habit to write the church letters of encouragement, instruction, and exhortation. It is from these letters we know he was ready to be 'poured out.' He was, in fact, not only ready; he *longed* to be poured out. So, let us, rejoicing with him, hear his familiar voice, and let us heed it. Let us hear an exhortation from Paul's own hand, regarding the body and blood of our Lord:

> Having therefore, brethren, boldness to enter into the holiest by the blood of Jesus, by a new and living way, which he consecrated for us, through the veil, his flesh; And having an high priest over the house of God;
>
> Let us draw near with a true heart in full assurance of faith, having our hearts sprinkled from an evil conscience, and our bodies washed with pure water.
>
> Let us hold fast the profession of our faith without wavering; (for he is faithful that promised;) And
>
> Let us consider one another to provoke unto love and to good works: Not forsaking the assembling of ourselves together, as the manner of some is; but exhorting one another.

"So now let us exhort and provoke one another, as Brother Paul wished us to do, to love, and to good works, and to faith, so our hearts do not become hard. These are difficult times and are made even more difficult because of this grievous loss. So, let us, indeed, assemble together, for we *need* one another. And let us *love* one another, as he so often encouraged us, because Christ first loved us. And let us *forgive* one another, for, and Brother Paul knew *this* all too well"—there erupted polite laughter of appreciation for my daring to exploit for the sake of levity our Brother Paul's frequent need for forgiveness—"*we are forgiven as we forgive.*"

"When we returned from Hispania, fewer than three weeks ago, standing on the docks at Ostia, Paul made me promise to write a testimony regarding the life of our Lord. For some reason he thought the church would profit if I were to add my recollections to those of Apostle Mark, whose recent letter has been distributed in the churches from Jerusalem to Corinth. But I vow to you today, literally, on his grave, I will go one step further, in honor of our fallen brother. I pledge to you today, to honor Paul with a history of the early years, which recounts his missionary journeys." The mourners applauded and hearty "Amens" rang out across the meadow. Somebody needed to recount Apostle Paul's trials and travels as an evangelist of Christ, and "Brother Luke was just the one to do it," all agreed.

Nobody had accompanied Paul more than I, in fact, in many ways, Paul could not have done what he did without my care. The stonings and beatings had taken such a toll.

"One of the stories, the most appropriate on this particular occasion, I should think, happened in a synagogue in Antioch. (Not the Antioch where Paul went to the aid of our Brother Barnabas, when he went to the town of Paul's birth, Tarsus, to retrieve him. They labored together there another entire year. [I winked at Silas, as I quipped, "Did you realize that is where we were first called 'Christians'?"—polite laughter.]) "It was in *Pisidian* Antioch. We were traveling through all of Pamphylia and Pisidia, spreading the good news of Jesus and Paul was compelled to visit the synagogue. He was called to preach to the Gentiles, it is true, but he never, ever gave up on his people. *They* gave up on *him*."

"So, we were in the synagogue on Shabbat, and Paul preached a sermon; did the whole thing in *kai* structure (just to amuse himself, I presume!—more chuckles, but outright laughter from Barnabas, as he remembered). Do you know, he had so much impact in Antioch, the next Sabbath, nearly the *entire city* was gathered at that synagogue? It was a miracle of God. But when the Jews saw the multitudes, they were filled with envy, and contradicted Paul's teaching, even blaspheming. So when they'd had quite enough of their babbling, this is what Paul and Barnabas boldly said unto them:

> It was necessary that the word of God should first have been spoken to you: but seeing ye put it from you, and judge yourselves unworthy of everlasting life, lo, we turn to the Gentiles. For the Lord commanded us, "I have set thee to be a light of the Gentiles, that thou shouldest be for salvation unto the ends of the earth.

Some turned and made eye contact with Barnabas, as if to ask, "you actually said that? *To their faces?* While surrounded?" I continued, "And so they left that region, but I returned to Jerusalem. The remainder of that trip was quite eventful, as I'm sure we all realize. Paul and Barnabas were worshipped! The crowd nearly sacrificed to them! Ha! Just imagine! A wave of laughter, barely contained, coursed through the assembly. "Then who shows up but some of the Jews from Pisidian Antioch and Iconium, and made a great disturbance. The same crowd who worshipped them, now stoned poor Brother Paul and left him for dead outside the city gate. They gathered Paul and made their way back to their home church in Antioch. Not long afterward, Paul went to Achaia and, despite various trials and hardships, partly in response to a plea from Brother Hierotheus[2] here (gesturing in his direction) he resolved to someday go to Spain. But God, in His wisdom, did not fulfill Paul's desire to 'take the gospel to the Far Western Shore of the World,' until this very Spring. (By the way, Brother Barnabas, came from Hierotheus" hometown's and they will return directly to continue the work. They have need of support, so if you are able to help, please see them after we conclude. They are laboring there, along with Apollos and Aristarchus, up in Gaul, confirming new members." Applause. "We have no idea if Apollos and Aristarchus even know of Paul's fate.")[3]

And so, when last we met at Lucina's, we all processed to the port, where we laborers set sail for Tarraco, to tend God's vineyard. Those were the most fulfilling, eventful thirty days of my life.

We now committed the body to the earth, recited prayers, sang a Psalm and adjourned. Silas pulled me aside, his steely gray eyes bored into mine, underscoring the gravity he wished to communicate: "Brother, if it is disturbances you wish to avoid, do *not* publish a word about what you all just accomplished in Hispania Tarraconensis. People will die." I said nothing but nodded agreement and bit my lower lip, letting him know I appreciated what was at stake. Nero was eager to capitalize on the traumatizing effect of Paul's sudden and merciless slaying. Until Christ returned for His Bride, we would have to exercise utmost caution and discretion, or we would all pay. "I certainly do not want to endanger our new leaders," I said. "Their zeal exposes them." Silas agreed, nodding, "It does." "We need to get word to them, tomorrow, regarding Brother Paul's fate, may he rest in peace. And we need to pray Nero's designs against the church come to naught." "Amen."

2. Otto F. A. Meinardus notes, "Hierotheus, a convert of Paul's is said to have been baptized in Achaia by Paul and begged him to come share the gospel in his hometown of Astigi," deep in the interior of Hispania, down the *Via Herculea*, in Baetica Province. ("Paul's Missionary Trip to Spain: Tradition and Folklore," *The Biblical Archaeologist*, June 1978, 63.)

3. Aristarchus had, in fact heard of Paul's fate. He returned from Tarraco two days after the funeral. The very day he showed his face in Rome he was rearrested, tried for treason and martyred the next day. There was nothing Zenas could do, this time.

3

Off to Spain

(TWO MONTHS EARLIER . . .)

"Blessed be the Name of the Lord! Blessed be the God of Israel! Hear O Israel! Our God is One! Holy, Holy, Holy is the Lamb for sinners slain. Yeshua! Ha Mashiach! I thank You, Dear Father, that You have kept me this night, safe from all harm, that I may serve You yet another day. Place Your holy angel before me. Let all my words and deeds please You this day. Amen."

The prisoner, awake but, absorbed in his morning devotion, was not yet ready to open his eyes. His imagination was engaged elsewhere. Down the alley a rooster crowd from the perch where, each morning, he announced the dawn of a new day. The prisoner continued his prayer,

> Hear my cry, O God;
> Attend to my prayer.
> From the end of the earth I will cry to Thee,
> ["from the *end of the earth*!" With the realization that today is the day, comes a smile.]
> When my heart is overwhelmed;
> Lead me to the rock that is higher than I.
> For Thou hast been a shelter for me,
> A strong tower from the enemy.
> I will abide in Thy tabernacle forever;
> I will trust in the shelter of Thy wings.
> He sits up, raises his hands heavenward, his eyes still closed.

"Father in Heaven, Hallowed be Thy Name.

Thy Kingdom come, Thy will be done

As in heaven, So on earth.

Supply us this day all we need.

And forgive us as we forgive others.

Lead us not into temptation,

But deliver us from the evil one. Amen.

Slowly, deliberately, savoring the moment, he opens his eyes. The familiar, dingy ceiling; cracked stucco, cobwebs, damp and soot-stained, greets him as it has for months, with cold indifference. He smiles nonetheless. "We give thanks for the roof over our head," now praying aloud. "Thank You for teaching me to be content in whatever circumstance I find myself." Inhale. Hold it. Slowly, exhale. Rolling, with a little grunt, to a seated position on the rancid straw mattress, he arranges his tunic and vest, slowly straps on his sandals, one at a time, with much difficulty, then, with a bit of a rocking motion, manages to stand. After briefly assessing his chances of remaining upright, he continues, 'Thank You, Heavenly Father, that these old bones still support me after all they've endured! Thrice these old bones were left for dead. Shipwrecked, stoned, . . . well, 'Thank You, Lord' Ha, You know! Theophilus jumps to offer a hand to the wobbly gentleman, but he was too slow. The venerable one manages himself to shuffle to the table, then sits on the old, broken down stool, which is also wobbly and decrepit. Theophilus follows, offering subtle support, right hand to his elbow, left hand outstretched, just in case he loses his balance altogether. "Morning, Brother Paul!"

"Morning, Theophilus!"

The guard unbars the door. "There you are," with a bow and a courtly gesture. Then, with a wink and a nod, "Free for a time and no place to go, I suppose. . . ." "On the contrary," said Paul, rubbing the muscles that ached and working his ankles in a circular motion, squinting in the direction of his warder. "I've friends due any minute. Meantime, I'll wash myself in the fountain just down the way. Please, my boy, tell them where I've gone, should they arrive before I return?" "Certainly."

I arrived just as Paul was struggling to get under way, still rubbing his wrists.

Nearly breathless, from both exertion and exhilaration Timothy managed, "I hope he's still sleeping! I want to see his expression!" His breath is visible on this cool spring morning.

"Are you kidding?" chided Barnabas. "He's likely grown impatient and set out without us! HA!" "Do you think," asked Timothy, "he'll be surprised by all this support?" jingling the bag of silver and gold coins in his ochre *maniakis* waistcoat, "by such a large number prepared to follow him to the end of the earth?"

"I hope so. I hope he feels less abandoned," replied Barnabas. "He realizes how generous are the saints in Rome, but this is beyond imagining. . . ." Both men smiled, shook their heads and picked up the pace. They were positively giddy. As they rounded the corner and crossed the street, a few blocks away, here stood Zenas the Lawyer, leaning against a physician's rooms, one foot resting against the wall, enjoying the morning, polishing off a steamy cup of tea. "Greetings, Brother Zenas," both said in unison. He grinned, but never broke his gaze toward Paul, who was just finishing his morning "bath." I waved and offered a jaunty, "Brothers!"

Barnabas yelled, more loudly than he ought to have, "Brother Paul, you are a sight for sore eyes! Paul and I both clucked. I offered a hand and we walked toward the others, Paul, concluding a thought: "Zenas has done well, brother Luke. Without his help I would never have been departing this day for Hispania." Timothy added, in his usual, chipper tone, "Nor I!" "Nor I," Aristarchus was also newly released. Both bowed and thanked him in unison. The counselor simply placed his tea cup on the ledge beside him, and nodded his welcome; shunting aside their praises of his lawyering skills. Zenas gave God all the glory, all the time. Paul said, "Let's go!" In the blink of an eye, we were down the street, some of us went to the briefing, others to the outfitter's.

There were ground rules to observe, expectations, and various instructions. The briefing took nearly a half-day. We had to pay a bond that, sadly, drained the bag in Timothy's waistcoat. I paid what we lacked. The clerk assured us most of the deposit would be returned if Paul appeared for sentencing on the agreed upon date. Most importantly, we learned that the leave was limited to 30-days only, not a minute more. (Zenas had asked for *sixty* days.) So we had barely enough time to evangelize Spain. And, with regard to evangelization, Paul was explicitly instructed to "speak to no one in the name of his God." These parameters weighed heavily on Paul. He resented the state meddling with the work of God; placing roadblocks.

Regardless, as was his habit, he determined to follow God rather than man. Under the order of counsel, however, he smiled, nodded, and said nothing. He did, however, give his word to return for sentencing in 30 days. That he *could* do. Being the 15th day of Aprilis, we would have optimal sailing weather, so that was to our advantage. We would travel to the far shore and back under mostly clear skies. Still, it would take a miracle.

"Thanks be to God. We will work with what we have been granted." I interjected, "I wish we'd been granted another 30 days. This pace could do you in." I had concerns. I placed my hand on Paul's back, monitoring his breathing and the rhythm of his heart. Paul muttered, so as not to disturb his physician's intense concentration, and spat out, "Or, it could *help*. . . ." He had a bit of a smirk on his face. I tilted my head to the floor, eyes closed, focusing, feeling even more acutely, I acquiesced, "Yes, I suppose the fresh air could do you some good."

"It's all the same to me," Paul voiced his usual ambivalence about continuing in this life. "God's will be done." Having taken my readings, satisfied for now, I picked up my bag, winked, nodded at Zenas, and gestured at Timothy to gather Paul's things, from where they'd been neatly stacked, in the corner of the proconsul's offices. We set out for the outfitters near the port of Ostia. While we had been in the briefing, several people had gathered, anxious to see us off; to impart some gift. "Timothy," Paul hailed his friend over the din, outside the offices, "be a good lad and run ahead to Lucina's. Tell her we'll be there after we check in with the ship's captain, and that we may have thirty for supper. She'd better plan for forty!" "Yes, sir. How far was that again?" "Just under a mile. On the right. Look for the iron gate with a lion on it. Just wait there for us and lend her a hand. Clement should be there waiting. Take a couple more lads with you."

"Yes, sir," replied Timothy. He turned heel and disappeared into the dust and the orange ripple of afternoon sun. It felt good, after his imprisonment, to feel the sun on his face for more than a few minutes at a time. Paul began to take another step and halted. He had caught a whiff of what he believed to be loaves of Lucina's delicious bread, emanating from her kitchen, even at this great distance. He took another deep breath, closed his eyes and imagined the warmth, the honey and oil. He was likely just imagining it, hungry as he was. He hadn't taken time to eat since morning. Assuming the business at the docks didn't take too long, the sun would set shortly after they arrived at Lucina's. His pace, unsteady as it was, quickened noticeably. I chuckled to myself. "I told him to eat. He never listens."

4

Three Days in Ostia

Brother Marcus walked into town, calling out, hands cupped, inviting and entertaining: "Come hear a man, jailed for his beliefs, teach about the kingdom to come! Admission is free!

"Why listen to a jailbird?" shouted a rowdy passerby. "He's probably a Jew."

"He is, at that. By birth, but that is not what his message is about, Sir."

"Probably stirring up trouble" exclaimed another peddler, struggling under the weight of his vegetable cart. But he had energy for one more barb, "Where is this circus taking place? I have some rotting vegetables that need a good home!" Several nearby guffawed.

"Down by the Tiber River, come as you please. Down by the Tiber River, one big family! If you're all alone, you won't be long. Just bring your lunch, we'll sing some songs. Down by the Tiber River, everybody follow me!"

"But, Sir, *where* on the Tiber River is this so-called family gathering?"

"Within a stone's throw of the port . . . Ostia city limits."

"Bring your friends! Come hear the most wonderful teaching ever to grace the Empire!"

The only visible reaction Marcus could discern on the faces of those within ear shot was utter rejection and contempt. He did catch a cordial glance now and then, however fleeting. "There is a Christian," he thought to himself. "I'll see him latter. No doubt!"

The deacons had found a piazza situated on the banks of the Tiber, a short distance from Lucina's place. The prelate (sympathetic to The Way) allowed us to utilize the space, as long as we promised to "clean up after yourselves and do not embarrass me." Paul paced back and forth, amongst John Mark, Barnabas, Apollos, Zenas, Onesimus, Timothy, Epaphras, Justus, Aristarchus and myself. People were congregating. A hushed murmur mingled with the babbling of the Tiber, 30 meters away, behind the beautifully symmetrical sacred grove, with its statuary astride the boulders beyond the spectacular green into which the piazza was integrated. Paul decided to preach and teach (or, rather, *to teach*—he had been instructed to not preach his "sacrilege") from a large flat spot on one of the boulders that held no statue, but was wonderfully framed by two large Corinthian columns.

Apollos estimated, "We have room for five, maybe six hundred. 100 are gathered now." John Mark, nodded. He thought the space was adequate. "We may find a better location, a bit more secluded; prying eyes may be less of a problem. But the acoustics would not be nearly as good as they are here." The others concurred. We had permission and we were out of the city. We should be fine. The wall that jutted out from the columns, along with the concave surface of the granite boulder would amplify Paul's voice beautifully. Yes, this would do. A crowd larger than 500 seemed unlikely on such late notice.

But word had started to spread the previous Sabbath. Many were now drawn to Ostia to send off the party who would finally evangelize Hispania. Apparently, the church at large was as excited about the mission as was the Apostle himself. Some arrived on horseback, some by ox cart, on foot, some by boat, down the Tiber, to the harbor at Ostia. So Paul decided, the most profitable way to spend the time required to outfit the party and secure passage to Spain, was to confirm in the faith those who came. "If the Holy Spirit gathers them," said the Apostle, "He must want me to teach them." He hated waiting, by nature, so pouring himself into these lambs seemed the most faithful use of that otherwise "wasted time." He turned to me and nodded to his left, indicating he wished to have my ear. We walked a few paces and Paul said, "Please pray with me, Brother Luke." We asked for God's guidance and blessing, then Paul shared his thoughts regarding the sessions: "I think it would be good to launch the ministry of the Word relative to the spirit of this place. In other words, after we pray, after corporate confession and absolution, then readings from Torah, and some singing, I think I should explicate the Three Pillars: Religio, Pietas, and Numina. It would be a very small step, then, to segue to my epistle to the church in Rome, no?" "Indeed, that sounds like a wonderful tack," said

I. "Alright, then. Pray God's blessing. Thank you, brother! You are always so amenable!" "Thank YOU, brother. You are always so eloquent." As we slowly walked back toward the other brethren, Paul replied, "Ha! I don't know about that. . . ."

"Er, John Mark, I need you to do something for me, post haste." "Yes, sir?" "There is a synagogue up the Via Severniana." "Yes, I know it." "Good," said Paul. "Please go see if they have midweek services. We need to get up there before the ship departs." John Mark asked, "Any particular time, Brother? When do you expect to have a break in these sessions?" "I'm not sure of that. Let's just find out when they meet and we will formulate a plan." "Yes, sir. I will return before lunch." "Very good. And see if there is any word from Titus?" "Yes, sir. All we have managed to learn thus far is that he is somewhere on Crete!" Paul mumbled to himself that he already knew that much.

A number of brethren were charged with attending to the myriad practical arrangements entailed in a missionary expedition of the magnitude envisioned. He fully intended to exploit the enthusiasm Christians far and wide had demonstrated at hearing of Paul's release from house arrest, and also that he was actually going to realize his long delayed dream of evangelizing Hispania. This would be a grand undertaking, financed by the generosity of the whole church, across the empire, and beyond. No doubt, whomever came to these special meetings would be especially eager to support the work of the 10 brothers committed to the month-long mission.
It was time to begin. The brethren gather around Paul, join hands and pray, then, at Paul's behest, Barnabas and Apollos offer prayers and read scripture. Epaphras, Timothy, and Aristarchus helped with seating arrangements and waiting on the assembly; Luke, Zenas, and Onesimus attended to Paul; arranging scrolls and tablets, fetching water, and waiting. I thought Paul's color was not quite right; I would keep a close eye on him.

Once the Psalmody concluded, two young, muscular brethren helped Paul up to the platform hewn in the rock between the pillars. A handful of doves fluttered about on the breeze that emanated from the Tiber, rustling the new growth on the trees in the grove. Wild flowers dotted the courtyard and perfumed the air. "God's beautiful creation," Paul's voice positively boomed as he signaled that the lesson would now commence. The sound quality was excellent! The crowd hushed, save for a few fussy infants. Given that it *was* just midday, the size of the crowd surprised him.

"God's magnificent creation clearly shows us God's ways and His works, for His invisible attributes are clearly seen in what He has made. God's magnificent creation clearly shows forth His glory and His Godhead. Hence, the 'Three Pillars': Religio, Pietas, Numina."

Some were startled to hear this notable Christian teacher grant, here at the outset, so much legitimacy to Roman religion. Others waited to see where he would take it. Most didn't even understand the connection. But this little buffoon amused them and they hoped there would be bread. They were there to be entertained . . . and fed.

"Religio, Pietas, Numina. That is, 'faith, duty, spirit.' Repeat that, please." All echoed, "Faith, duty, spirit." "Faith, duty, and spirit are pillars, not only of the Roman religion, but of the worship of Messiah Jesus of Nazareth. I will elaborate this contention, showing you by means of our holy writings and some passages I have composed in recent months, during my imprisonment. Oh yes, I have been under arrest in Rome these past two years, and I have not been idle!" The crowd was amused by Paul's self-deprecation. "Oh, so you *are* a jailbird. I thought that was a joke!" People looked around to see who it was that was being so insolent, hiding in the back there. Paul took it in stride. "Yes, I have been imprisoned and chained, beaten *and* left for dead, more than once. Why? What crimes have I committed?" "*None!*" came the vehement but unsolicited response from the Believers in attendance. The question had been rhetorical.

"Oh, but I did commit crimes, in the eyes of the state. I preach an outlawed deity. This is no mean indictment and here I am, in fact, at it again! Ha!" "Some people never learn!" The rude, unkempt person in the back of the crowd was not the only heckler in attendance! "Ha! Did I claim to be a quick learner? No!" Laughter ensued. Paul had passed the "does he take himself too seriously" test. "But I have promised to be on my best behavior today, and however long it takes for us to board our ship for Hispania." The interest generated by the mere mention of that exotic land was palpable. "Yes. As soon as we are able, 9 of my brothers and I will board that ship, just beyond the frigate, past the far dock," people strained to catch a glimpse of the ship to which he pointed, "and spend the next 30 days spreading the good news of Jesus of Nazareth to the ends of the world, to Brigantium, on the far Western shore of Hispania. Or, rather, *they* will. I am just along to, to, uh . . . delivering famine relief." His sly wink elicited a few sniggers. Now he had their full attention.

"And what will 'they' tell them? They will tell them that 'Religio, Pietas, and Numina' are all grounded in the One Who Made All Things. In *Psalms of David* it is written,"

> *The Lord said unto my Lord, Sit thou at my right hand, until I make thine enemies thy footstool. . . . The Lord hath sworn, and will not repent, Thou art a priest for ever after the order of Melchizedek.*

"The Lord said unto my Lord." This Lord was with the Great Lord in the beginning. Through Him were all things made, in Heaven and on Earth. He came to earth to reign as a priest forever 'after the order of Melchizedek.' The Majestic Lord has sworn, and will not repent. He swore He would do it, and He did. God is invisible, but He made himself visible. He sent us Jesus of Nazareth. Jesus is our Great High Priest. He is God's only son and he came to show us the Father. There is a line from a famous song,

> *Faith is the evidence of things not seen.*

What does this mean? Look at the beauty all around us! Flowers, trees, birds, water. These are all signs of God's love. Did you realize you are made mostly of water? Water around you, water above you, water inside you and you, inside the waters of baptism. It is into the waters of baptism that you will go if you wish to be born again of the Spirit of God Eternal. This is what Jesus, the High Priest after the order of Melchizedek, has said.

> *Repent and be baptized and you shall receive the Holy Spirit.*

What does this mean? He is the author of our faith. He has made clear our duty: repent and be baptized. Jesus taught that we are to love one another. And it is the Spirit that gives us the love we give.

Numina. Spirit. God is Spirit and they who worship Him must worship in Spirit, and in Truth. Above all else, we must not "worship created things over the Creator." (Paul enunciated, slowly, for effect, the latter clause, pausing as he gazed off in the distance at the statuary on the far eastern end of the piazza.) Returning to the point of origin, he deliberately made eye contact with many along the path of his eyes, and again with an unnerving, cadence, 'Our God is a jealous God.' So it is our duty to love Him and Him alone, *and* to love our neighbor as He has loved us. This is what our High Priest teaches us of . . . say it! The crowd eagerly obliged, "Faith, Duty, Spirit!"

Paul concluded his lesson by stressing that their duty to one another is to love as we have been loved. He elaborated on true piety, to follow God's design, not to pervert it as so many do. "But He is invisible, how can we know?"

"We know. We know, friends. He shows forth His will through what He has made and the Word spoken by the Son whom He sent to show us The Way. He has been very clear with us. We have been warned, in fact. Many, though they know He is God, glorify him not, neither are these thankful. They become twisted; their foolish hearts are darkened. Professing themselves to be wise, they became fools, and changed the glory of the incorruptible God into an image made like to corruptible man; to birds, and four-footed beasts, and creeping things. So God also gave them up to uncleanness through the lusts of their own hearts! Do not, my friends, change the truth of God for a lie! Do not worship and serve the creature more than the Creator! It is our duty to love and serve, trust and obey Him. And, in turn, He commands us to love our neighbor as He first loved us, expecting nothing in return. We owe God perfect obedience because Jesus was perfectly obedient, unto death. But, in ourselves, we are incapable even of less than perfect obedience. This too is a free gift from our merciful Father in Heaven. This obedience the Holy Spirit supplies. He has made Him Lord! He has made Him our High Priest, Blessed forever, Amen! Faith: *He does it.* As the Psalmist makes clear. Duty: Love one another . . . *He gives the Love we give!* Spirit: He gives freely of His Spirit to all who repent and are baptized. *He gives!* Faith! He gives! Duty! He gives! His Spirit! Say it."

The call and response went on for some time. Paul then made an elegant amplification; beginning with a few practical exhortations about life together, and finished up a short hour later. His crescendo was simply teeming with couplets. We took up an offering to support the mission trip, invite those in attendance to return, and broke for lunch. Several were disappointed, disgusted really, as they were instructed to go find food in the nearby market. But food was scarce in those days. They were really expecting a handout. So, we heard a lot of grumbling.

Others hurried home to gather all the loaves and wheels of cheese and bags of tea they could get their hands on, eager to make some denarii. We were about to leave when John Mark returned from the synagogue. He reported that there was but one service per week, until Pentecost. Paul slowed his pace and looked to his traveling companion, "Timothy, son." "Yes, my lord?" "Lucina said something about a lunch. Could you please run ahead and check on that for us? I expected it would be delivered to the piazza. Perhaps I misunderstood. I am famished. If they are on their way, I would just as soon eat here."

Timothy said nothing, but when he turned to do Paul's bidding, his way was blocked by a group of young acolytes who had been scouring the markets and docks for various provisions. These approached and Servius, a sandy-haired lad who was possessed of a modicum of courage, whispered to me that the food shortages were making it more difficult than they anticipated to find provisions. I broke the news to Paul as delicately as one could.

"Well," he growled, "I suppose, when I finish here with the teaching, I could go and find some figs and apples and a few barrels of water. Maybe even some salted meat. Would you all enjoy some salted meat? I can skip my evening meal!"

"I'm sure that won't be necessary, brother," I said, trying to smooth things over. Ach. That thick blood. Paul wished to impress on the young men that they were expected to fulfill their charge without bothering him. Servius managed, with trepidation, "Sir, we have searched every. . . ." Paul's demeanor, and color, stopped Servius dead in his tracks. Wisely, he ventured no further excuses. (He was possessed, apparently, also with a modicum of wisdom!) Paul, realizing his bluster and his stony glance had had the desired effect, softening his tone considerably, placed his hand on Servius's shoulder and advised, "You boys go now, with Timothy to Lucina's. Ask Lucina for names of friends who might help us. Timothy, could you teach these youngsters how to provision a mission trip? You have the most experience with this sort of thing." "Yes, sir. Right away." Timothy shot the boys a somewhat condescending glance. "This is not the last time you will hear this from me, friends." Paul raised his voice so he would not have to repeat himself, looking around, "We have only a very short time to meet an ambitious goal. I must return here 29 days from today. If you wish to help us, bless you. But meeting a goal of this nature, in so few days will require of each person involved, every bit of resolve he can muster; every bit of strength he has got; and there will be no time for relaxing until the day we return." One had to wonder if he were giving himself a talking to. Paul was ashen. As the young apprentices fell into line behind Timothy and gingerly headed for Lucina's, I placed my hand on Paul's shoulder and shot him a look of concern, the "concerned physician's look," but said nothing. Paul got the hint and responded with uncommon deference: "I need rest. Let us resume the lessons in two hours." Epaphras and Aristarchus sprang into action, informing those who remained what was the plan and asking them to please spread the word. Half of them never returned.

Paul introduced, after the midday break, a discussion of the things of the Spirit, from the earliest passages of his recently published letter to the Roman Christians. With reference to the Roman idea of Numina, Rabbi Paul stressed how the things of the Spirit must be understood by means of God's Spirit, and that, only through repentance and baptism, by the means God had provided, could they understand the things of the Spirit. When he approached the part of that letter devoted to the Jews, about circumcision and the old covenant, he opted rather, the following day, to elucidate for those assembled (and the number dwindled, somewhat—the word was out, "no cake to be had at *this* circus!"—still, more Believers had arrived, anxious to send off the missionary party) "the difference between spiritual things of God and spiritualism, which is superstitious and idolatrous." However, provisions were eventually procured (many of which were donated by the Believers; they had not arrived in Ostia empty-handed!) While Paul did not wish to be disturbed with questions about provisions and support, he was, on the other hand, by nature attentive to minutiae! So, every once in a while, the teaching was interrupted long enough for Paul to offer an opinion or make a suggestion. Most times he took these interruptions in stride, but there was an occasional outburst. These were well-contained, being "center stage" as he was. As cranky as Brother Paul could be, he never wished to be a stumbling block, especially to new converts. And there were new converts. At close of the second day on the piazza, we walked down to the Tiber and baptized nearly 50 converts. This was a remarkable number, since the times were so dangerous. But, in reality, we had attracted very little attention. The main boulevard was several hundred feet from our gathering, and the grove made a good veil. And I think God must have protected us from harm, because none befell us. Paul had been warned in his briefing that he was to refrain from evangelizing . . . so he stuck to teaching and let the rest of our disciples shepherd those who wished to join The Way. Paul's color improved.

Those few who returned were rewarded. Barnabas spoke above the din. When the crowd realized he was talking logistics they quieted down and heard of the company's plans for the departure from Ostia: "Well, friends, the sky is red, as you see, so we will be here one more day. Let us adjourn for the day and meet here again, tomorrow, 1 hour past morning prayer. We have some travel arrangements to deal with, then Brother Paul will teach again. Go, have dinner, sleep well and we will see you tomorrow." Timothy quickly whispered something in his ear. "May I have your attention? Please. Please, all, listen to me. If you have no food, or are unable to purchase food, some provision has been made, through the generosity of our host, Sister Lucina and her friends. So, follow us back to Lucina's and limited rations will be distributed." Applause and giving of thanks. "If you already have made plans for food and lodging, and have plenty, please allow the sisters to care for the less fortunate. And, of course, if you are a person of means, please invite those around you to break bread with you at your lodgings, and we will see you in the morning!" All departed, in good cheer and in anticipation of Paul's lecture, for they were all aware this could be the last time they heard him teach this side of heaven.

Lucina was such a grand lady of the Church! The lunches she provided were first rate. But the evening meals were an event! Lucina's home cooking was second to none . . . and that Italian food! There was nothing like it under the sun. We had noodles and tomato sauce and sausages and pomegranates and the most wonderful bread, from wheat ground on the premises. Lucina's demeanor was saintly in every way, at all times. The tender care and hospitality she extended to all, including her servants, was beautiful, as was her home. She kept her estate tidy, but not immaculate, lived in, but not unkempt. She had nice things, but they were only things. It was obvious, by the love she gave, people were her treasures. She was a jovial and extroverted widow. She laughed a great deal, with a deep, throaty and booming laugh, from the depths of her substantial belly! She was filled with the joy of the Lord. Her salt and pepper hair, kept off her face with a fat, single braid that reached to her lower back, framed raven eyes, huge, dark eyebrows, and lashes to match, set pleasantly in olive skin that had a clear, smooth, complexion. Yes, Lucina was full of life, confident both in her faith and in her prosperity, but humble; she lived to serve others. And this evening, she was in her glory!

The night before we left (we left on Day Three) Lucina served us shrimp and noodles, salat caprese, wine, sausages wrapped in cabbage leaves, biscotti and dark Arabic cardamom tea, some other kind of new-fangled salad, and lemon torta, spaghetti Bolognese topped off with Spanish red wine (imported specially, to inaugurate our mission journey) and chocolate cake with strawberries. What with all the singing and stories and clinking of goblets, the meal took 3 hours and, before bed, right there at table, we all sang Evening Prayer. It was midnight and there was no further talk, only the strong desire, felt by all, to get horizontal and savor the fruits of Lucina's hospitality.

Next morning was Shabbat and Paul yearned to visit the storied new synagogue up Via Severiana. He was positive he could exploit recent events (things were not going well in Jerusalem) to the furtherance of the Gospel. He freshened himself, grabbed his traveling copy of his letter to the Roman Christians, and made his way to the kitchen table to discuss further with Lucina her question from the evening before, regarding law and gospel. Since she and her scullery maids would be busily preparing breakfast he thought, perhaps, he could pull her aside, let them handle the preparations, and he could have her undivided attention for ten minutes or so, and explain the juxtaposition of "law and liberty in Christ" over another cup of that envigorating Mauratanian cardamom dark tea! Drat! Apollos was already there. "So much for enjoying time alone with Lucina . . . " he mumbled to himself, breaking into a polite smile, nodding "Good Morning."

True to form, Apollos dominated the chit-chat over tea. Through much "back-and-forth" he and Paul decided a trip to the synagogue was out of the question this particular morning, because, due to uncertainty about the weather, it was decided the crowd sleeping about Lucina's grounds should be directed in morning prayer then they could all process to the boat. The boat was expected to set sail mid-afternoon, so they expected they would have time only for some good-byes and some final exhortations . . . and to take one final offering. We were *not* in this for the money, but it takes money to sustain ten individuals, in a foreign country, for 27 days. It takes quite a little money! By then we had raised about half the money we anticipated we would need to conduct the mission trip Paul envisioned, so it was imperative to draw as big a crowd as possible and implore them to help support the endeavor. So Paul, partly to get people in motion and partly to carve out a moment alone with Lucina, asked Apollos to go roust the others. "Tell them we plan to get underway within the hour. Tell them to bring their friends!" Apollos took the hint. "And Apollos," Paul added, "please find me a clean papyrus and a good writing kit. If I cannot make synagogue, I will write my kinsmen a farewell letter. This missionary trip will provide all the inspiration I need! And see if you can find Clement! He's going to miss the boat!" Paul shouted as Apollos disappeared around the corner.

Lucina filled his cup, pushed the honey jar closer, set down the tea pot, then set herself down beside him, grabbing a handful of dates and placing them on a cloth in front of her. She offered Paul some, but he patted his belly to indicate he had no room for dates and sighed, "Well, I am disappointed we will have no time to walk your grounds, but I agree with Apollos: I must get back to the souls out there." "The synagogue will keep," she nodded, spitting out a pit and taking up another date. "I don't know why you bother with them, anyway." Lucina was not known for tact. "Because they are my *kinsmen*" Paul insisted. He blew in the cup, then took a contemplative, slow, two-handed, sip. "Lucina. Do you . . . " he hesitated. She looked up, spitting a pit, or rather, letting it roll off her lower lip, into her hand. "Do you ever . . . " he really was reticent to begin the day in this fashion.

"Brother Paul. You know you can ask me anything. Please. . . ." Emboldened, Paul took a deep breath and asked, without reserve, "Do you ever allow persons to bury their loved ones on your property?" Lucina was a little taken aback, if not disappointed. It was indeed not the sort of concern one expects to be confronted with on the morning after such a festive, wonderful evening. "Ummm . . . nobody has ever asked." "Lucina," he explained, leaning closer so as not to involve the maids, "when I return from Spain, Nero will pronounce sentence. This is it for me." She gasped at his morbidity, whispering, nonetheless, to avoid upsetting the help, "No! No, Paul. You were only just set free! "I was not 'set free,' dear heart," with arched eyebrows and a sad grin he clarified for his dear friend, "I was granted a leave from house arrest on the condition that I return for sentencing. I gave my word to return after concluding so-called 'business' in Spain." "Yes," she pleaded, "but I assumed you would stay in Hispania; maybe disappear?" He only shook his head, slowly, sadly, from side to side, and broke eye contact, then replied with steadfast resolve, "I gave my word."

A solitary tear trickled down her cheek. She remained silent. The discussion regarding law and liberty never took place. Preemptively, Paul arose, excusing himself, with a feigned note of seriousness, "I shall go prepare the morning devotion. See you in 15 minutes, out back." He hadn't time to console her. She will get used to the idea. He headed for his room.

"No visit to the synagogue," he thought to himself. That aggravated him to no end. But, he thought, "If my letter to the Hebrews turns out *half* as good as the one to the Roman Christians. . . ." He shook himself, and exclaimed, "No! It shall be my *greatest* work!" As his end approached, Paul was consumed by the desire to leave a legacy. It was not pride that motivated; it had more to do with a desire to serve; to be spent, rather, in service to God. And he was compelled to share the word of faith with his kinsmen, despite their contempt for him.

After devotions, while the processional was forming, Apollos approached Paul, setting him back on his heels with enthusiasm. "If I were allowed to speak in synagogue I would certainly reason with them from *Psalms*!" "Yes, well, believe you me, it is no holiday, young man! I have had more trouble than I care to recount, reasoning with that 'stiff-necked people'!"

Apollos, decided he needed to exhort his elder, "'Seventy times seven,' brother. 'Seventy times seven.'" "Apollos," Paul lost his patience, just a bit, "have you ever been stoned and left for dead?" "No." "Exactly. I will write them a letter. And it will be poignant and powerful and apropos." Apollos, almost taking the bait (I had given him "the eye," he was enthusiastic, but not stupid!) quipped, "Ha! I see what you did there." Paul played along. "The old man can alliterate with the best of them, still. . . ." "Indeed he can," Apollos politely conceded, though his tone belied his belief that his was a more fetching style.

"Chancel-prancing little peacock" Paul thought, disdainfully. Immediately, he repented, and simultaneously chuckled at his naughtiness. Clement never did show up. Having no real choice, Paul reluctantly asked that I invite Apollos to replace the young apprentice who was, apparently, lost in Rome. Apollos was a man of means. We needed his "deep pockets."

We sang morning prayers in Lucina's olive grove, then processed to the port, where Paul gave a final message as our provisions were loaded. "We go to the Gentiles in the farthest reaches of the world. This is Christ's great command. We follow it. We are happy to obey! But what does this mean for the Children of Israel? Are they not blessed of God? What benefit hath the Jew? Much in every way. The covenant of Abraham was fulfilled in the Jew. God chose to deal directly with the Nation of Israel. Messiah came from the Nation of Israel. Jesus called his disciples from the Nation of Israel. But they crucified Him, the Lamb of God, slain for the sins of the world! So, now He has turned to the Gentiles. . . ."

And Paul spoke for about an hour more, regarding the call he had received to preach to the Gentiles, and how he had dreamt of sharing the Gospel in Hispania, and how God, through Brother Zenas, had procured his release, for these 30 days, "Well," said he, "we now have fewer days, only 27, so we had better be off!" The crowd roared their approval and their support. Earnest prayers were offered, final gifts received, and we set sail for Hispania.

5

Paul Seeks Wise Counsel

THAT ENTIRE FIRST DAY at sea, Paul stayed below. Now it was evening, and he went topside to get some air and to think. Leaning against the ship's rail, he was lost in the gorgeous traces of orange, white, purple, and pink, dazzling splashes of luminescence layered across a vivid cyan canvas. He savors the cool ocean breeze, its clean, salty drafts reviving him with each deep breath. He basks in the warmth that envelopes his too pale body. It was all such a welcome contrast to the stench of his cabin below decks! Gulls scavenged and bid farewell to the sun as it sunk into the perfectly calm Great Sea.[1] Thanks be to God! And thanks be to God for the written word! Exhale, slowly.

What of this epistle? He leaned against the bulwark, taking in the glories of the sea, meditating on the majesty of the Creator of the heavens, the seas, and all that is therein. What of this dangerous game they're playing back home in Judea? Could he somehow influence . . . Apollos assumed he had been working on the manuscript (the assumption was confirmed when, as he approached, he noticed the ink stains on Paul's fingers). "Brother, Paul!" Apollos's approach, from his right, just behind, wrenched Paul from his musings. It was unwelcome.

"I was in my room most of the day, with a chamber pot nearby. Came up for a bit of fresh air and to celebrate the calm! What an evening, eh?" "Yes, finally. The seas were a bit rough today" Paul, seeing no escape, responded politely. "I've seen worse." "Where have you been?" Apollos, as

---

1. "Great Sea" is the name for the Mediterranean commonly used by 1st-Century Jewish folk.

was his habit, answered his own question. "I take it you're working at your writing?" Apollos was anxious to collaborate. "How is that coming along? Fairly well, I surmise, since I've not seen you all day! Ha!"

"God is good. I have a general outline, have completed a couple of lines of analysis, and have a few ideas for sailing metaphors. By God's grace I have weighed anchor and set sail." He immediately regretted giving Apollos an entrée. "Clever. That is good news! The Jewish Christians will prosper through your labor, both now and forever." "I'm not sure they'll even read it if they know I wrote it," Paul remarked, off-handedly, thinking out loud, more than anything else. Apollos jumped at the chance to provide unsolicited advice, fanning the embers of old tensions. Realizing the damage was already done, Paul proceeded, "I am faced with a dilemma: 'Should I or should I not affix my name to the letter?' Can't make up my mind." "I see. Why would you not?" This struck Apollos as odd.

Paul gave up all hope of a moment to himself; to mull over his own thoughts on the matter. "Still, Apollos, is eloquent. He may have some worthwhile insight," he thought. "I want this letter to my kinsmen to be my magnum opus. I want the tack to be different than any of the others. Hence, the sailing metaphors. I intend to invest a great deal of effort in it during this trip, because I do not expect to have much time to work on it when we return to Rome. I hope to dissuade them, as well, from continuing with this foolish revolt." "I see," replied Apollos, in a rare moment of concision. "But, why invest so much time and effort in a letter the Jewish Christians refuse to read?" Paul had dealt with them enough to realize there could very well be little to no readership, a thought he could not bear, given it would be his last. "Why on earth would they not?" Apollos knew the reason, but he was playing dumb because he wished to engage Paul on rhetorical aspects of his writing, where he was convinced he could make a substantive contribution. Flattery, he assumed, would secure an open ear.

"Well, two reasons, really. First, they hate me." "Oh, they do *not!*" "Yes. Yes, they do, Apollos. Many of them do." "But, why?" "They still hold against me the persecution I brought on them in the early years." "Oh. Well, as far as that goes . . . " Paul was not about to let Apollos dominate. " . . . and, second, if I attach my name to this document, I believe a number of the Hebrew Christians will refuse to read it because of their views regarding Gentiles." "You think those old prejudices hold sway amongst the Hebrew Christians, at large? I would think . . . " "Yes. It has been demonstrated to me time and time again, in various ways. Being 'Apostle to the Gentiles' has its own particular set of challenges" Paul noted, sadly. "Well, I think they're silly." "Thank you. Still . . . " Paul trailed off, weighing options, again. Of course Apollos would view the bias against Paul in this light; he is a Gentile.

"Ever since you asked me to fetch you those writing instruments, I cannot help but think what sorts of teaching you will include in the letter to your kinsmen! This is most exciting!" Paul simply nodded. "I should think that it will be difficult to get through to such a hard-hearted and stiff-necked people. Have you considered what sorts of stylistic elements you will employ, beyond the maritime metaphors?" "Probably the usual ones: parallelism, rhetorical questions, and syllogistic logic," Paul replied, mechanically, knowing full well what was to come. Here we go. . . .

Apollos made a lengthy, self-congratulatory suggestion regarding the use of parallelisms, in which he excelled, you see. "When it comes to breaking through that rough exterior, to speak to the heart, I would think strategic use of parallel structures will serve as a hammer, breaking away the shell. Anaphora would be very helpful in terms of establishing a rhythm that will give the entire fabric of the treatise a seamless quality . . . like a fine Persian tapestry. The refrain, once established, can be withheld for a season, then, once anticipation builds, re-introduce the refrain at just the right interval to underscore your most important point. Running metaphors are excellent, as well, when one wishes to compose a seamless argument. Seamless arguments demolish a hard shell like no other construction. They soften hard hearts! If you were to utilize, strategically, some sort of powerful idiom, building upon the motif, point, by point, you would surely penetrate the rough exterior, as you break away the shell. Repeat some phrase, strategically, throughout the piece. This will help weave the entire work together, and drive home whatever point is attached to the saying. It could be an exhortation or an aphorism or a proverb . . . say! or an *allegory*! And, beyond these, what sort of illustration would they relate to? I have given it much thought the past two days: Priesthood. Ever since the days of Aaron, Jews associate spiritual authority, above all else, with their priesthood. And what is the priesthood in which they invest supreme authority? You mentioned it in your lesson, in Ostia! Yes! The Priesthood of Melchizedek. I suggest a seamless discussion of Jesus as 'a Priest forever after the Order of Melchizedek!' This image, compounded and amplified by means of parallelism and antithesis, will surely stir a visceral response in the hearts of all Hebrew Christians! One thing is certain, is it not? It will take something special, even sublime, to stir the hearts of such a stiff-necked people? *Images* give impact!" Paul had got much more than he had bargained for, or was willing to endure. "Do you ever take a breath?"

"Excuse me?" "My dear Apollos, when I say I wish this to be my magnum opus, I do not intend to elevate the work, as a showman would, by means of superficial embellishments! This letter is not about my ability to paint flowery images and turn a brilliant phrase. I am not entering a speech contest! I am doing God's business; teaching God's people. The excellence I seek is attached to didactic strengths, not flowers and fancy!"

"But, Brother, I merely—" Paul cut him off. "Look. It would be too ostentatious for my purposes to embellish my instruction with any more metaphors, chiasms and antitheses than I already employ. I have my stock schemes and tropes; the ones I am in the habit of utilizing. They have served me well. What is needed is a more excellent message. Deeper truths. The 'strong meat' of the Word."

Apollos was not easily dissuaded. "Well, I pray you at least hear me on this one point: You should not comment on the rebellion. True, you will address Hebrews, but stick to the Gospel." But Paul did not even hear him. Paul had no problem discussing surface matters with Apollos. But, when it came to the substance of his letter, he had no idea what shape the final draft would take. And, honestly, ever since Ephesus, he held a rather low opinion of Apollos. Being a novice himself, Apollos had influenced the new converts both there, and later in Corinth, in such a way that Paul suspected he had antinomian tendencies. He certainly had a need to build a following. Paul grumbled to himself, "First he baptizes in the name of John, then *in his own name*, for goodness's sake!" His jaw was now clenched. "Should have left him in Rome. This is going to be another disaster," he thought to himself. He took another deep breath of the fresh air, to calm his blood.

"I am toying with the idea of an opening movement something like, 'Wherefore, holy brethren, consider Christ Jesus, the Creator of heaven and seas and all therein.' . . . 'Consider Him who is worthy of all honor.' No. 'Consider Jesus, whom the very heavens and seas obey.'" Apollos hazarded a suggestion here, also. "How about, 'Consider Jesus, the High Priest of our faith'? That he wrote the covenant, so to speak, in his holy blood?" "Yes." Paul saw some merit in the idea. "I should expound the meaning of our faith for the sake of a people who are likely to misunderstand its basis and be blinded to its merits because of their traditional ways of thinking about matters of faith. And, it would be good, also, to point out that Jesus is not only the Author, but the Finisher of our faith! Faith is not completed through the works of our hands. He both authors and finishes it." "Yes! This is most certainly true!"

Apollos was energized. Paul had taken a suggestion. He had more. Many more. "With regard to the parallelisms, I've been thinking. Since hearing the Word of God is prevented by hardness of heart, perhaps you could repeat the words, 'Today, if you hear His Word' or 'You must hear His Word Today!' I believe there is a scrip—." Paul had to cut him off. He was seething. "That does not take it in the direction I intend, Brother Apollos. Sailing metaphors. I want sailing metaphors."

Oblivious, he continued right along: "But it seems to me the logical tack would be, within the context of the solution to hardened hearts, would be a turn toward Moses and the wandering in the wilderness. Address them as the children of Israel, then mention the Covenant of promise, the hardening of the hearts, hearing His Holy Word, and so on. Do you see the dialectic?" "I see a lot of empty words and rhetoric." Apollos heard this snide comment. "Empty words? These words have such potential to move the souls of the readers that they are changed forever! I thought you wanted this to be your magnum opus?" "I do. However, we do not judge excellence by the same measure." "Sure we do!" Apollos was about to wish he had held his tongue. "You wish to have posterity think well of your work, because of its excellence; its vivacity, perspicuity, its sublimity!" "Aha! Do you not hear yourself, Apollos? I am less interested in taking credit for the work than in writing as I am moved by God's Spirit. You think of composition as a high achievement of man's imagination." "I think it is important, Paul, not to take credit for the work, but to accept ownership, as it were, for one's *teaching*. Of course the objective is to follow God's lead . . . " Paul shut him down; pulled rank.

"Yes. I'm sure that is your only concern. Your motives are always pure, when it comes to ensuring your name continues. I am sure you had nothing to do with the factions that developed in Corinth." Paul could no longer contain his distaste for Apollos's pomposity, his grasping ways, his proclivity for self-aggrandizement. Apollos did not appreciate the implication. But he ignored it. "I baptized *no one* in my own name. Not a single soul. That was the product of some over-zealous converts. I, point of fact, found their actions distasteful and embarrassing and put an end to it!" Paul snorted, "After how long did you put a stop to it!? After your status had already been secured!" Apollos sighed heavily. Now *he* was exasperated. "We've been over this, Brother. Let's get back to your manuscript. I can imagine a nice parallel con—" "No. Let's not." Paul shut down the conversation, turned on his heel and walked away, mumbling, "Why, oh why, could Clement not have. . . ."

"What's that?"

"Nothing!"

"Brother Paul!"

Apollos yells, in part to be heard over the ocean and the pesky, importunate gulls, in part, because he has tired of this ill-treatment from one who was supposed to be spiritually mature.

"For the record, brother: *I do not consider you a rival.*"

Paul harrumphed and disappeared behind a large spool of halyard.

6

Formulating a "Battle Plan"

THE BRETHREN GATHERED FOR a light breakfast, in the galley, at six bells. They enjoyed the biscuits, fruit and boiled eggs Lucina and Claudia had provided. They were so generous, and the oranges were particularly delicious! Barely a word was spoken between them, but, after washing down the victuals with copious amounts of sweet dark tea made savory with cardamom, Paul announced, "Our aim this morning is to formulate a plan for spreading the good news in Hispania. We will be in country precisely twenty days. We need to be about the Master's business, stay focused, identify indigenous leaders, and Luke, Zenas and I will need to return to Rome so I may discover my fate." They were all business; all full of anticipation for the adventure ahead, but all anxious about what lay ahead for their apostle. "Let us pray."

"Blessed be the Name of the Lord! Blessed be the God of Israel! Hear O Israel! Our God is One! Holy, Holy, Holy is the Lamb for sinners slain. Blessed be His Name! Yeshua! Ha Mashiach! I thank You, Dear Father, that You have kept me this night, safe from all harm, that I may serve You yet another day. Place Your holy angel before me. Let all my words and deeds please You this day. Amen."

> Hear my cry, O God;
> Attend to my prayer.
> From the end of the earth I will cry to You,
> When my heart is overwhelmed;
> Lead me to the rock that is higher than I.

> For You have been a shelter for me,
>
> A strong tower from the enemy.
>
> I will abide in Your tabernacle forever;
>
> I will trust in the shelter of Your wings.
>
> Father in Heaven, Hallowed be Thy Name.
>
> Thy Kingdom come, Thy will be done
>
> As in heaven, So on earth.
>
> Supply us this day all our needs.
>
> And forgive us as we forgive others.
>
> Lead us not into temptation,
>
> But deliver us from the evil one. Amen.

"Dear Father in Heaven, please give us grace and wisdom to approach the work you have given us in a timely and methodical fashion. Bring us into contact with those souls whom Thou hast deigned to join your kingdom at this time. Work all things according to the excellence of Thy will. In the Precious and Holy Name of Jesus, under whose banner we sail. Amen." All said, in unison, "Amen."

"Brother Luke has been gathering anecdotes from the earliest of our efforts and has a faithful account of Cephas's Pentecost speech based on Prophet Joel. I thought it would be apropos to meditate on it this morning. Luke?"

Luke cleared his throat, tilted his scroll toward the weak morning light now illuminating the portal, closed his eyes for a brief moment, praying, then took a breath and began:

> And in the last days it shall be, God declares,
>
> that I will pour out my Spirit on all flesh,
>
> and your sons and your daughters shall prophesy,
>
> and your young men shall see visions,
>
> and your old men shall dream dreams;
>
> even on my male servants and female servants
>
> in those days I will pour out my Spirit, and they shall prophesy.
>
> And I will show wonders in the heavens above
>
> and signs on the earth below, blood,
>
> and fire,
>
> and vapor of smoke;
>
> the sun shall be turned to darkness and the moon to blood,

before the day of the Lord comes, the great and magnificent day.

And it shall come to pass that everyone who calls upon the name of the Lord shall be saved.

"He went on to compare Christ with David," Luke elaborated, "to demonstrate to the multitude that God had made the one whom they crucified both Lord and Christ. They were cut to the heart and asked what they could do. Peter told them to repent and be baptized and assured them they would receive the gift of the Holy Spirit. For the promise is for you and for your children and for all who are far off, everyone whom the Lord our God calls to himself."

"Thank you, brother Luke. ' . . . and for all who are far off.' ' . . . for all who are far off,' he repeated for emphasis, then let the words reverberate within the galley. "Day after tomorrow we shall arrive in Tarraco, and ten days later, will stand on the Far Shores of the world. The 'ends of the earth.'" This, too, he let sink in. "Thanks be to God!" "Lord, grant us grace!" "Amen."

"Ah," Onesimus interrupted. "Excuse me, but, as I recall, Cephas's remarks were somewhat more extended. I definitely remember him exhorting the crowd to, 'Save yourselves from this crooked generation,' or something to that effect?" "Yes, son, you are correct," I responded, with an affectionate, fatherly smile. "There were many other words. He bore witness at length, but I have spoken this morning only those that seemed relevant to our present aims." "Forgive me." Onesimus was embarrassed, took a step back, and tried to disappear.

Paul was, in fact, growing impatient for having been thrown off track. I made one more attempt at a charitable gesture: "I understand, Onesimus, you are gifted with an extraordinary ability to recall detail, especially when it comes to teaching, scripture, and sermons." "Yes, sir. I am." "We will talk after this meeting," said I to the novice. Onesimus nodded, not daring to prolong this distraction one second longer, thereby making himself a target. Paul was menacing.

"Ahem," Paul cleared his throat. "Right. So, here's what's needed: There are enough in our company to form five teams." "Um, sir," interrupted, Timothy. "That is no longer the case." He said, sheepishly, because he did not wish to tattle, "Clement did not make the boat." "Clement did not make the boat?" Paul was incredulous, but said nothing, except, "well, perhaps it would make sense to have four rather than five teams?" All agreed; strength

35

in numbers and all. Two-by-two was the ideal, but they were bound for a lawless frontier. Anything could happen.

"So," Paul continued, "thanks to Brother Clement, we are nine. Have you given any thought to those with whom you would like to travel?" "It depends," Timothy interjected. "Are we still intending to cover all the major coastal cities in twenty days?" "Yes," several chimed in. "It seems to me," his index finger traced the proposed cities on the map he spread on the table before them, "disembarking in Tarraco, then fanning out to Narbo, Burdigala, Valentia, Nova Carthago, Corduba, Gades, Felicitas Iulia and Brigantium is quite enough ground to cover in 20 days! Ambitious, yes. But, if we focus on the coast," as he gestured, the map rolled back to its original shape, "with God's blessing, we can avoid the mountains; trust the new leaders to evangelize the interior. The team that heads for Brigantium must spend a few days in Caesaraugusta, don't you think?" "Excuse me, sir," Barnabas spoke up for the first time, "I believe the ship makes a brief stop in Narbo, does it not?" "Ach! Yes. I had forgotten," exclaimed Timothy. Paul jumped in, "So, 'Team Alpha,' let us call it, disembarks in Narbo, proceeds to Burdigala, then returns to Tarraco by way of Caesaraugusta. I'm not sure how many of you realize this, brethren, but, when I was last in Antioch . . . "

Paul continued as Zenas unfurled the map and splayed it out on the now cleared cedar table. He anchored three corners with pewter mugs. There were only three empty mugs. Zenas looked around and, on a nearby counter sat a serving tray and, on the tray, a bone-handled iron bread knife. He stuck the knife into the fourth corner, with a little too much vigor, and it made a loud "twang!" After having made eye contact with a number of the brothers, smirking, to confirm his action had had the desired dramatic effect, Zenas slid the lantern closer.

" . . . when I was last in Antioch, I baptized a zealous young Spanish boy, Hierotheus" (the name elicited nods of recognition from a handful of the passengers.) "Hierotheus made me promise that, if we made it to Hispania, we would evangelize his hometown of Astigi, which is, I believe, in Baetica Province, near Corduba. It is imperative to me that I make good on that promise. There will be a single opportunity." "Let it be so" arose the unanimous agreement.

"Brother Paul," I ventured, cautiously; tentatively. "Perhaps we could reach more people, in the time allotted, if we focus our efforts on the Tarraconensis, then leave some behind, whose schedules allow them to spend more than 20 days? They could 'work the fields,' so to speak: identify indigenous leaders, teach and baptize, ordain bishops, maybe even establish a school? Tarraconensis is the most populous part of Hispania and has better roads, besides."

"I do not wish to limit our mission objective to one region only. The entire purpose of this trip," Paul argued, "is to cover the *whole* country!" All were silent. "God has impressed upon me . . . " Apollos was whispering in Timothy's ear, behind Paul's back, not daring a direct challenge, still smarting as he was from last evening's verbal thrashing. "Brother," Timothy was *not* shy about interrupting, "is our objective to cover ground or save souls?" Paul snapped, "Both. I have no time for your false dilemmas. Both!" "Granted, Sir," Timothy proceeded, cautiously, but also made bold to repeat the question, because he sensed agreement amongst the brethren who understood where he was taking the discussion (they had learned to follow Timothy's lead when it came to dealing with Paul): "If we take advantage of the improved roads, which will allow us to spend more time confirming in the faith the converts God gathers to us, and charge them, before they return home, to make new disciples in the remainder of the lands we—."

"Very well," Paul waived him off, because he saw the wisdom in Timothy's [but, really, Apollos's] suggestion. (One wonders if Paul would have assented had the idea been voiced by Apollos.) All redirected their gaze to the map. The morning sun now streamed brilliantly through the portal and, conveniently, fell directly on the map. Timothy blew out the lantern.

Paul hunched over the map, deep in thought. He half mumbled to himself, "Yes, it will be understood, part of our aim, that those who remain, after I return to Rome, will not leave Hispania until a counsel is held and the new elders submit their plan for spreading the gospel. . . ." Accommodation was difficult for poor Brother Paul. He now stared blankly at the map. Just as Timothy was about to jump in, yet again, I, as is my habit, intervened. I had a very sensible plan in mind. "What if we have three teams of three, to divide cleanly our number? . . . Teams Alpha, Beta, and Gamma. "Team Alpha" can disembark in Narbo, day after tomorrow, and spend twenty days evangelizing extreme Southern Gaul, along this loop, here, up the Via Aquitania, through Tolosa, to Burdigala, then, down here, toward Caesaraugusta, and returning to the rally point, at Tarraco. Apollos and Onesimus, you had intended to go that direction, yes?" "Yes." "Who would like to join them?"

Timothy, eager to move along the process, made eye contact with Barnabas, who, almost imperceptibly nodded his permission. "Good," he thought to himself, "Timothy can keep an eye on Apollos." Timothy, in turn, nodded at me. "Timothy, then" says I. "Question," blurted Epaphras. "Yes?" "When 'Team Alpha' disembarks in Narbo, should they begin spreading the gospel immediately, or do we have contacts in these various towns, or is the objective to move as quickl-" "Brother Epaphras," Paul barked, "can we please stick to the general plan at this time and discuss the finer details in our next meeting? I believe we will frustrate the overall objective if we begin, right away, focusing on minutiae." "Of course. Forgive me."

I attempted to bring the preliminary phase of the discussion to a conclusion: "Team Alpha goes from Narbo, through Tolosa, to Burdigala, then returns to Tarraco by way of Caesaraugusta. "Team Beta should consist of Paul, Zenas, and myself, for obvious reasons." "Certainly." (Paul may have need of a lawyer; Paul definitely has need of a physician.) "And, in keeping with Brother Paul's desire," I made a mad dash to try and bring our preplanning to a conclusion, I was getting sea sick, so, if I didn't make a mad dash now, I would make one later! "It makes sense that Team Beta proceed down the Via Herculea all the way to Corduba, and, of course, stopping in Astigi, by way of Nova Carthago?" "Certain—" But Paul interrupted.

"The culmination," he over-enunciated for effect, " . . . of my life's work is to go to the ends of the earth. The. World. Ends. At. Brigantium." Paul asserted his status and slowly looked around the table, head cocked, *argumentum ex silentio*. Oblivious, Aristarchus shot a puzzled look and asked, "So, sticking to the coastal regions is imperative?" All eyes turned to him, and in unison the answer came, "Yes!" We all agreed the interior would take care of itself; that we could only cover so much of the country in 30 days, minus 10 for travel to and from Ostia. But that was beside the point. I quickly integrated into the plan Paul's *fait accompli*. "Team Beta will proceed, then, up the Via Domitia all the way through Caesaraugusta to Brigantium, then return to Tarraco on day 20." Aristarchus chimed in, "Maybe Team Alpha and Team Beta could join up in Caesaraugusta for the return leg to Tarraco?" "That's a possibility," that made sense, and besides, Aristarchus needed some encouragement.

"This leaves Barnabas as team leader for "Team Gamma." Aristarchus, you and Epaphras join forces with Brother Barnabas, hightail it from Tarraco to Valentia, then Nova Carthago, then Corduba and return to Tarraco by the twentieth day." Aristarchus whistled to indicate what was obvious to all: they had been given a tall order, indeed. "Is that practicable" wondered Barnabas out loud? "Ach! You have strength to spare," I exclaimed, in jest! "Be men about it! Go! *Make disciples*!" Barnabas feigned being unnerved and, with his fingers, made a sign like a cross. Everyone had a good laugh. Aristarchus and Epaphras slapped each other on the back and all agreed that, being young, Team Gamma could move more quickly than the others, and besides, all three were available to stay beyond the 30-days allotted to Paul, Zenas, and myself. Still, it was a *tall* order.

"Well, we have a plan. Let us pray" I said, deeply satisfied. "Brother Paul?" Paul prayed; Barnabas reassured Paul his team would, God willing, go to Astigi. All agreed to meet again after noon meal to work out details. Paul made a final point as the meeting adjourned: "Brothers, gather no support from any convert in Hispania. The love gifts gathered in Rome and Ostia will easily cover the costs of this mission. God be praised, we even have enough support for the first indigenous leaders until such time that they are able to become self-supporting."

"Thanks be to God!"

7

In Tarraco

THE CROSSING WAS UNEVENTFUL. When they landed in Narbo, Team Alpha, consisting of Apollos, Onesimus and Barnabas struck out for Burdigala in Gaul. They were eager to begin evangelizing, so, right there on the docks, before the ship even took on cargo bound for Tarraco, Apollos stood on a bale of Persian rugs and began holding forth. Most of the remainder of the missionary party leaned over the rail and encouraged him. Some heckled! It was a joyful moment of release for men confined mostly below decks for four solid days, albeit irreverent! Then again, the crew was a vulgar lot, so the frivolity probably captured their attention! Men from other ships didn't quite know what to make of it, but found it oddly appealing; entertaining, at the least. In between high adventures, theirs was a dreary existence. Paul thought their conduct distracting and rather silly, but he left them to it. He had business at his writing table. This time at dock would be perfect writing time. The entire company gathered on the dock, at eventide, after Apollos had finished horsing around, and sent Team Alpha off with prayer, bid them Godspeed, and all chanted The Song of Simeon:

> *Nunc dimittis servum tuum, Domine, secundum verbum tuum in pace:*
> *Quia viderunt oculi mei salutare tuum*
> *Quod parasti ante faciem omnium populorum:*
> *Lumen ad revelationem gentium, et gloriam plebis tuae Israel.*

Lord, now lettest Thou Thy servant depart in peace, according to Thy Word.

Now mine eyes have seen Thy salvation which Thou hast prepared before the face of all people.

A light to lighten the gentiles, and the glory of Thy people Israel

They took on cargo and fresh water, and set out for the brief jaunt to Tarraco. They landed sometime after midnight.

The missionaries disembarked at first light, ate a lovely, hot breakfast near the port, sang morning devotions, and prayed for safe travels. They decided that this special circumstance warranted chanting again the Nunc Dimittis. Paul blessed them, and sent Team Gamma down the Via Herculea to Valentia. He made them promise to go to Astigi on his behalf. Paul was intent on fulfilling the promise he had made to Hierotheus, at his baptism in Achaia. He said he had never encountered such a pure zeal and deep love for the souls of one's countrymen than he had in Hierotheus. Yes. He would fulfill that promise, so help him, God. But the Proconsul had left them so little time. Paul sighed, picked up his satchel and staff, and got himself moving.

We immediately turned our attention to the business at hand. It was a glorious morning! A pattern of thin, golden clouds streaked the pale blue as if by the very fingers of God, in neat, symmetrical undulations, spanning one end of the heavens to the other. Unusually downy clouds of purple, white and gray bordered the golden furrows, accentuating the horizon. It would be a warm day, but the mariners were all expecting heavy rains. As we discussed God's grandeur, standing against the doorpost of a nearby shop, two girls looked up at the sky, having obviously taken a cue from our conversation. Paul greeted them as he took a few steps in their direction, "A beautiful morning, is it not?" "Yes, father," said both, in unison, demurely.

These were stunning young ladies, barely twenty years of age. They appeared to be sisters, probably Greek. The one who appeared to be the elder of the two had darker, fuller, features. She was a handsome young lady, and quite confident. Her confidence added to her beauty. The younger was stunning. This lass had lighter features, light brown, wavy and fulsome hair, that shone with a slightly red hue in the morning sun, a perfect, creamy complexion and eyes of green/brown with yellow flares, encircled by dark accent rings. They wore traveling clothes, neat but functional, and walking shoes. Both carried packs; a third was on the ground next to them. They were not travelling alone. That was a relief. The bold one apologized, "Sorry to have listened to your conversation, but it was difficult to not! You certainly know how to appreciate the handiwork of the gods!" Paul was defenseless against their charms.

"What is your name, child?" "I am Xanthippe and this is my little sister, Polyxene. Our brother, Diocles, is inside, getting directions to our uncle's homestead in Toletum." The younger sister, kept silent, never looking up. Always on her guard, looking slightly uncomfortable at the approach of strange men, she adjusted her scarf and glanced toward the shop door. "Well, Xanthippe, you are a bright young lass. We are indeed in the habit of appreciating God's grandeur, and of helping others do the same."

"Excuse me, sir, you forgot to give your name." "Ach! I did. I beg your pardon. I am Paul of Antioch. This is my physician, Luke, and our friend and brother, Zenas. We are, in fact, here in service to God Almighty." "Oh! Wonderful! The God of the Jews? You are Jewish? You look very Jewish!" Polyxene giggled under her breath at such impertinence. "Indeed I am, child. You are observant . . . and er, inquisitive!" All laughed at Paul's teasing. Both girls blushed.

A concerned looking bearded young man, dressed in traveling clothes, came crashing through the doorway, assessing the situation as he stepped into the street, a cheese in either hand, a bottle and bread wrapped in cloth, under his arm. Meeting Polyxene's eyes, he turned to his other sister, "Xanthippe! Why are you talking with these *Christians*?" he packed a lot of disdain into those syllables. He had watched from inside. Paul asked calmly, "And this must be brother Didolys?" Xanthippe answered, "Diocles. Yes." Turning to the others, "Brother, this is—"

Diocles cut a striking figure. He was perhaps five or seven years older than the girls, a big, strapping lad, a head taller than Zenas; two heads taller than Paul. His hair was raven, his eyes looked like two onyx stones, perfectly positioned on either side of the bridge of his nose, half-way between his eye brows and his cheeks. His beard was well-groomed. His cloak, leggings, and the dagger in his belt, suggested that he had served in the military. He was ready for action. "I *know* them" he declared. Heard their babbling back home, when I was younger than you two." "Ahhh . . . and where was home?" inquired Zenas, attempting to defuse the situation. "Psidian Antioch." "Of course," I added. "We were there four, maybe five, years ago, wasn't it?" Paul and Zenas agreed.

"Brother, why are you being rude?" asked Xanthippe. "They have been nothing but gentlemanly." "They are all trouble. All of them. Especially this one," pointing to Paul. Paul smirked. Here we go! "This is the ringleader of them all. When they came to Antioch, he turned the whole town upside down. Including our parents' household." Diocles was bitter.

"Well, I am sorry for your misfortune, Diocles," Paul said, sincerely. "We never intend to stir up trouble, but it certainly follows us, that I cannot deny. It is part of the cross I have been given to bear." "Yes, I'm sure it has nothing to do with your seditious teachings," Diocles said, sarcastically. I could see this was going nowhere, so I interjected, "Say, we are looking for the market square, can you direct us? Then we'll be on our way."

"No." Diocles, despite the censuring stares emanating from *both* sisters, was disinclined to extend courtesies to this band of troublemakers. They were, no doubt, recruiting for their revolt. He picked up his pack, put it on, and continued, "We are just passing through. Ask someone else. We have to go to the stable down the street." Zenas mentioned that we, too, needed to hire a cart. As it turns out, the stable was directly on the way to the marketplace, the "Emporion." Xanthippe and Polyxene both realized as much, they also knew enough of the layout of Tarraco, despite their brother's vehement objections, to help us find our way. The day before they had visited the place and purchased a few items for their journey. Both girls invited us to join them for the half-mile trek to the stable. Their elder brother's contempt had only piqued the interest of the girls in this trio of kind and gentle rabbis.

As they walked, they talked of faith, the men asked if the youth knew of any "followers of The Way" in Tarraco. The girls surmised that the elder gentleman, Paul, wished to teach lessons upon entering each successive town, *all the way to Brigantium*. They asked how such a venerable gentleman supposed he could make such a trip, Paul replied that he had been all over the world. At this, it dawned on the girls to whom they were speaking. They quickly adopted an attitude of deep respect for the fabled Brother Paul, "Apostle to all Hellas." His stature, but also his demeanor, commanded great respect. The outfitter was quite busy and, after fifteen or so minutes, Zenas said, gauging the position of the sun, "It's time to eat. Is anybody else hungry?" Xanthippe said, only yesterday, they had dined at a lovely café on the northwest corner of the Emporion. The girls volunteered to show us the way. "Polyxene! You need to stay with me! Let your pigheaded sister go, if she must, but you stay here." He knew better than to try and reason with the elder of the two. "Poly" was a bit more compliant, or, at least, less stubborn. But Polyxene apparently had a stronger will than her brother realized! "No, brother. I will go with them. I have *questions*." She walked over and joined us. All looked to Diocles. He stamped off into the stable, positively shouting, "Do *not* make me wait! Once we have a cart, we must ride for Toletum!" He was all business. The girls grinned, wheeled around, each took one of my arms, and led the way to the Emporion.

"You are bound for Toletum?" asked Zenas. "Yes, sir. We are going to work for our uncle. Things are too difficult back home. We seek better fortune here in Hispania Tarraconensis." "So, you will travel through Caesaraugusta?" the lawyer asked. "Yes. We leave first thing in the morning. We intend to spend the rest of the day preparing, sleep in an inn near the via, the Via, er . . . " Polyxene was stuck, not having travelled much. "Via Augusta?" "Yes. Via Augusta. We will travel to Caesaraugusta, then turn Southwest to Toletum." "Mmmm." The coincidence was lost on no one.

Tarraco was a nice sized town, even as Provincial Capitals go. There was a lot of new growth; several shops, newly painted. Vendors congregated in the street outside their stalls, drinking tea, sunning themselves, and passing the time, nattering about politics and the weather. We passed a stately looking music hall, with grand columns all around the portico, and newly installed statuary, as well. Tarraco was busy; trade just gathering momentum for the season. Shoppers, peddlers, potters, artisans, apprentices, carpenters, freighters with their laden carts, and aristocrats doing business in the seat of commerce for the province, all intermingled on the busy cobblestone streets. It took a long while to navigate past The Praetorium. There was some sort of goings on that attracted a large crowd, making it difficult to pass. Fortunately, every street in this part of town was paved and had a walkway. It could have been worse.

About half a mile past The Praetorium, after dodging many a donkey cart and avoiding countless beggars, we turned a corner and spied a bustling, expansive city square, the Emporion! The girls halted, got their bearings, then "It's right over there," Xanthippe pointed away off to the northwest corner. "Do you see it? It is just to the right of the Provincial Forum." I couldn't see it. Zenas asked, "Is it just beyond the blue tent, there?" "No, no." Polyxene, pointed just to the right, "over in the corner, *red* sign, *across* from the Forum. See it?" "Yes. There it is!" Zenas, who had grown hungry since they had disembarked, took two steps in the direction of the café, then stopped when he realized no one else had followed. The girls did not intend to eat with us, despite the fact we had invited them several times since the stable.

"You are more than kind," said Xanthippe, "but Diocles expects us back. He's surely finished by now, probably mad as can be. He worries about us." "Girls, you have a good brother." Paul had been scheming to himself as we walked. "What are the chances you can convince Diocles to let us travel with you to Caesaraugusta? We have to go that way to get to Brigantium, and, if I am not mistaken, Toletum is a short distance south from Caesaraugusta on a fine, new road. They've only just completed it!" "That is how Diocles described it, yes."

"Brother Paul, surely we need to spend a few days in Tarraco?" Zenas interjected. "Not necessarily, sir." Paul had already considered it. "We will return to Rome via Tarraco, so I am inclined to think, perhaps, the Lord would have us proceed, with haste, to Brigantium, then focus on spreading the gospel all the way back to Tarraco. We have so little time. And we will have this afternoon to look for Christians with whom we can meet on our way back. No?" "Yes. That makes sense, Brother." Zenas could think of other approaches, but he yielded. This was *his* lifelong passion, after all, and, as far as spreading the Good News, he could imagine no "soil" being more prepared to receive the seed of God's Word better than was the soil of these girls's hearts. He just ached to get on with the business at hand. That, and he was starving!

"Perhaps we could even help with the cost of your cart?" Paul turned back to the girls. "We will have to see," Xanthippe replied, doubtful. Diocles was a cautious sort. "I will talk him into it," said Polyxene, with a twinkle in her luminescent grey-green eyes and a wry little smile framed by huge dimples. They would have to pass the Emporion to catch the road to Caesaraugusta, so we agreed to keep an eye out for them, and see what had been decided by then. They had a couple errands to run, so we expected to have more than an hour for lunch.

The girls made it back to their brother in short order, determined to convince him to at least listen to the rabbis preach the gospel in Caesaraugusta. What harm would it do? They had no idea what a toll that so-called "good news" had taken upon their parents' marriage. Nothing but trouble. It was time he explained a few things to them.

"Team Beta" took a table under a particularly, old olive tree, and ordered up a fish and rice dish, olives, an assortment of cheeses, bread, fruit, and red wine. Waiting on our meal, we took in the sights, watched people, talked little and sipped tea. All were tired, it had been a long morning; not that productive, but we had shared the gospel with the girls and they seemed eager to hear more. God willing . . . As we waited for our snack, Paul, just for the sake of conversation, asked Zenas if he were glad he'd come on the trip.

"Most certainly! I am pleased as can be, if for no other reason than I get to spend time with you!" Paul replied, with a faint smile crossing his face, looking at an ant struggling with a crumb in the canal between two stones at the foot of the table, "Ha! I'm glad you are pleased, but I don't know . . . "

A chap at the next table leaned their way, apologetically directing his comment with hand to cheek, "Sir. I apologize for my impertinence, but I believe I recognize you. Are you not Paul of Antioch, the famous Christian rabbi?"

Not pleased with the interruption, but still, managing a cordial tone, "I cannot deny it!"

"I knew it! I saw you in Ephesus, years ago! When I was maybe eight or nine." Paul replied, "Yes, I was there, what? More than 10 years ago! You would have been very young." "I was with my parents. All I remember is there was a great commotion. People yelling in the marketplace, 'Great is Artemis of the Ephesians' for the longest time! You must have really aggravated them! Ha!"

"Ha! I seem to have that effect on people!"

Displaying a quick wit, the young man snapped back, "We are not unlike in that regard!" We had a good laugh.

"Do you know Apollos?! We saw him preach in Corinth on that trip! He was so eloquent. I've never forgotten his teaching!"

Paul nearly choked on his paella. "Yes. He is, in our missionary league, only he is, at the moment, on his way to Burdigala, in Gaul." Paul was still a bit agitated (or feeling guilty, perhaps,) by the recent run-in, with Apollos. Zenas provided cover, allowing Paul to regain composure, "Are you students?" Another of the lads said, "We are apprentice lawyers in the provincial courts." Zenas replied, "Really? I practice law." The third asked, "Really? Where? Rome, I suppose. Everyone knows your companion there was imprisoned in Rome. I expect that is why you are with him now, in case there are 'complications'?" "Yes, Rome, mostly. You are correct, sir. I pleaded Paul's case for release from house arrest sufficient for him to come to Hispania Tarraconensis and take care of some affairs prior to sentencing."

"Mmmm. So you are a condemned man?" asked the first. No one answered. Again, Zenas deflected, "I started out in Asia, Ephesus, actually, but my career did not gain momentum until I moved to Rome. Defending Christians from the lions, mostly." The second lad said, in jest, "Oh, interesting! Does that pay well?" These boys were witty and quite amiable.

Zenas now moved to the crux, "So, young man," pointing across the table to the boy who'd recognized Paul, "What was your name?" "Forgive us! I am Prosperus, this is my friend Maximus, and of course, the indomitable, Probus." In his best impersonation of a thespian, Probus dipped his head and gestured with his hand, "at your service!" He was a jovial sort, and very bold. "He will go far in the law," I thought to myself.

Our food had by now arrived and we had engaged the apprentice lawyers in conversation a good half-hour when Diocles, Xanthippe, and Polyxene rode by on their cart, down the street, about 150 feet away. Zenas ran out to check with them, to see if we would ride with them to Caesaraugusta. When he returned to the table, to report back, Probus leaned over and asked who were those exquisite creatures. "They are lovely! The elder girl, with the darker hair, looks a bit saucy!" We gave him no answer, but only objected to his forwardness, already relating to them, as we did, as though they were our daughters in the faith.

Diocles did not want us to ride along. He said the cart had too little room for the three of us. Zenas was able, however, to make arrangements with them to meet in the market square of Caesaraugusta at noon, four days hence. "Splendid," said Paul. "Now, where were we? Oh. Pleased to meet you, boys. It is true, I am Paul of Antioch. This is my traveling companion and lawyer, Zenas of Ephesus and he is my physician, Luke. Are you followers of Christ?" (Paul was bold to the point of recklessness. He never gave a thought to the possibility that his very public inquiries could cause grief to those who made a public profession. Long experience had made him indifferent to suffering for the Name of Christ, so he presumed any show of timidity was tantamount to "hiding one's light under a bushel." It never occurred to him that some of us are simply more guarded, by nature. It always made me wince.) "Not remotely!" exclaimed Maximus, his vanity getting the best of him. Probus could only chuckle under his breath, as he polished off his wine. He was a bit of a dandy. Prosperus nodded, sheepishly. His friends were shocked at his public admission. They had not known this about him, though Probus claimed he had had suspicions.

"So," Paul engaged Prosperus, while Zenas focused on the cock-sure Maximus. (Converting haughty skeptics like Maximus was sport for Zenas.) I ate an orange and listened to Probus go on about the girls (concentrating mostly on that orange. That was a *delicious* orange!) Zenas agreed to meet at the café the following morning, to "talk law." Paul and Prosperus agreed to meet so Paul could instruct the young man in the faith. Apparently, he had never really received much in the way of catechesis. Maximus proposed one caveat: "We will have to meet early, Zenas, over breakfast, because my master, Quintilian, needs me to do some research for him tomorrow, and we are to meet in between court appearances, over lunch. I should have a free hour, maybe two, after breakfast though, I think. Paul interrupts, "Wait! *The* Quintilian? You are apprenticed to Marcus Fabius Quintilianus?" "The very same! My master is presenting a closing argument, soon in fact, over in the Forum! You should come listen to him! He's a remarkable talent. Eloquent. Stunningly so. And a good man, besides."

Paul was not about to pass up this invitation to hear the most celebrated young speaker in the Empire! "Could I? I would enjoy that very much," the prospects of converting such a popular figure excited Paul like anything. He assured the apprentice he was a citizen. Maximus bragged, "I can get you access myself. And I'll introduce the two of you when court adjourns." "Wonderful!" Paul was up in an instant. We made eye contact, which implied, "please pay for lunch."

Paul, Zenas, and Maximus all went directly across the boulevard to the Forum. I was not welcome in the Forum, so I went ahead to the inn to arrange for rooms, before they filled up for the evening. Prosperus had to check some records at a Provincial Office near the Praetorium. I never saw Probus again (though Zenas tells me he swept Xanthippe off her feet!)

8

Paul and Quintilian Meet

"CITIZENS, THIS FINE FELLOW, Sabinus here, says he had the bad fortune to witness Naevius Apronianus 'strike the fatal blow' that took the life of his young, diminutive, defenseless wife, Fabiola. And what did we hear, by his previous account? That Naevius appeared to be intoxicated, that he was certainly, according to Sabinus's account, full of rage, 'out of control,' he says; 'beside himself.' That he 'willfully covered up his action,' and that, on subsequent occasions, 'he showed no signs of remorse.' These are all certainly damning indictments." ("Good," thought Paul, once he had gotten situated, at the rear of the courtroom, just behind the patricians, "he's just begun his peroration.")

"However, my fellow Romans, my examination of Sabinus clearly tells a different tale, paints a different picture. It should be quite clear to all that Sabinus's previous testimony was based on presuppositions regarding Naevius's appearance and that he even drew inferences about the innermost thoughts of the accused." Ironically, Quintilian was, at that moment, forming an erroneous opinion of the strange looking little old man whom, if he was not mistaken, had been led in by his own clerk! He would have a word with Maximus.

Quintilian was a smart looking young man, thought Paul, clad in first rate legal regalia, polished sandals and fine, well-manicured features. His jet-black wavy locks never were must, even though he frequently spun, about face, as he paced in front of the judges. His arms gesticulated with tanned limbs, apropos of a man who was both a gentleman farmer and an expert pleader, who abides over his legal craft with secure mastery. Marcus Fabius Quintilianus glided across the front of the assembly, prodigious voice booming, round, dark eyes piercing, securing the imminent release of the accused with each new refutation. A striking figure, especially considering he was just in his early twenties. He stared right at Paul as he feigned listening with rapt attention to Sabinus's testimony as the clerk read it back, ad nauseam. The reading was strategic; the staring, only a distraction.

"Who is that tramp with Maximus? Why has my clerk brought a tramp into my courtroom?" Quintilian wondered, silently to himself, in between sententiae. "Is he a citizen? He looks like a Jew." He was a little put out. "Yes, let the court hear more from the accuser's lips." For all his words, Sabinus had said absolutely nothing. He clearly had an obstructed view so, in his heightened emotional state, his fancy had supplied what was required to fill in gaps with suppositious "facts."

The strange Hebrew fellow—yes, he was clearly a Jew—made a poor first impression, still, there *was* something about him; a glint of intelligence in the eye, beneath the grubby exterior. "Intelligent or no, he looks silly there, seated so near the patricians, in his traveling tunic and cape. Hmmmph. Needs to learn his place." Still, Quintilian's interest was piqued. There was a second gentleman. He had an altogether different look about him; confident, good posture. He too appeared to be a traveler, but a better dressed one. He made an abrupt quarter-turn left and signaled with his hand for the clerk to stop. The flood of words, words, words, had done its work. "Is it not clear, gentlemen, good citizens of Rome, that this simple man before you, this unfortunate victim of circumstance, full of fear, overtaken with so much anguish he hid his eyes? Is it not clear that he then proceeds to swear by what he saw, misinterpreting so very many actions of poor Naevius's, ascribing madness to what we now know was grief; presuming to know motives, yea, the very turning of his affections, of his bowels of sorrow, one simply *must* doubt Sabinus's account of the death of Naevius's beloved. It is much more likely, as Naevius has repeatedly claimed, that his sweet, sad, bride, in sadness, threw herself out the cursed window, than that he had anything to do with it. He is no more guilty than a herdsman whose prize belled ram is taken down by wolves while the herdsman is off rescuing a lost sheep. In his deep remorse, and rage at the wolves' savagery, he may, indeed appear to take the blame; for he was not there to save and protect that which he is sworn to care for. But his anger at himself should not be construed as an admission of guilt, friends. And who would blame the herdsman for the treachery of a wolf? Indeed, one probably ought not even blame the wolf itself! Killing sheep is its nature! And, just because you, see the herdsman with the sheep in his arms, walking toward you, blood-stained and vexed, does not mean . . . " Paul listened with keen interest.

The droning of the witness notwithstanding, he had never observed such an orderly, decorous proceeding; more devoted to the cause of justice than to following the letter of statutes. He found the experience both exhilarating and utterly reasonable; the epitome of decent orderliness. Despite his having been so often at the mercy of Roman justice these past few years, he realized how much he appreciated these emerging codes for civil conduct, guided as they were by reason and truth. God's provision for law and order is truly a blessing, he thought, watching Quintilian fulfill his vocation brilliantly. He was undeniably eloquent. "I wonder if he possesses wisdom in keeping with that eloquence," Paul said to himself, under his breath, subconsciously comparing the pleader to Apollos, whom he considered a fop. The comparison was a natural one. Their styles were somewhat similar, approximating the Gorgianic, but Quintilian was more sober, less emotional. Indeed, Quintilian had a touch of sobriety, or rather, of substance, from which Apollos could learn! "Too bad the old boy is up in Burdig—" he didn't complete the thought before his inner dialogue broke out in objection! Whatever time we have together, thought Paul, I will enjoy it all the more if I can engage in *disputatio* with this young man, *alone*. I won't have to work quite so hard to get a word in!

Quintilian concluded his closing remarks; the judge adjourned for the day. A decision would be rendered in the morning and sentencing would follow. As the weary pleader gathered his notes and scrolls, Maximus meekly shuffled up to the counsel's table, his new friends in tow. The accused had already been removed under heavy guard. Introductions were made. Paul dispatched Zenas to fetch Luke so they could return to the Emperion, have some supper, then share the Good News afterward, near the fountain.

"Welcome to Tarraco. Will you be here long?" "No. We are off to Caesaraugusta at first light," Paul explained, "I fear we were not allowed much time in the province to conduct our business." Quintilian never wasted time. "And that business would be . . . ?"

"Well," Paul said, being somewhat guarded, "I am a tent maker." "I see." Quintilian was too astute to fall for that canard. "If you don't mind my asking, how a tent maker got so beat up?" "Ah, yes. You don't make a lot of small talk, do you?" "I am busy. Very busy." "I travel in rough places, speaking words that are often unpopular, especially with those whose livelihood is tied to worship of idols and temple worship. There is much wickedness in the hearts of men." "Don't I know it!" Quintilian had seen his fair share of wickedness. "So, you are a preacher. Had a few run-ins, have you?" This deliberate understatement amused Paul. He let out a belly laugh and replied, "Indeed! I have been stoned, beaten, jailed, lashed, left for dead, thrown off boats, more than once!" "Oh. A Christian." Quintilian associated beatings and persecutions and troublemaking with Christianity. "Why? Why on earth would anyone in his right mind choose such a path?" "I didn't. It chose me." Quintilian only shook his head. Paul shrugged. Quintilian asked again, more vehemently, "Why would a sane man persist in such folly, only to be rewarded with poverty and imprisonment?" Paul heard, clearly, the implication that he was mad. But Quintilian was not deriding Paul. He knew of this chap, all in Rome know of him, and, as a pleader, Quintilian asked out of curiosity regarding how on earth he would, if he were called to ever defend him, how he would go about it. Jews were all trouble. But this man was a Roman citizen, also. Quintilian was taken with the enormity of Paul's sacrifice. Thoughtfully, quietly, Paul said simply, "I persevere for no interest of my own, but all these pains I gladly suffer for the one who suffered, unto death, for me."

Quintilian was moved by such selflessness. To his core he was moved, but he didn't let on. His ambitious nature, just reaching full bloom as it was, caused him to mask such reactions. Paul read him, and understood. He remembered being of the same mind when he himself was young and ambitious. He would try a new approach. "Ironically, I was well on my way, prior to my conversion, to being a Hebrew among Hebrews. Like you, in my own country, I had the pedigree and credentials to lead an entire party, and was well down that path. But my God had different plans for me." Quintilian thought within himself, "Okay. Here we go. . . ."

"Yes. I remember hearing of you from an acquaintance. Tragic fall, that." Shrugging it off, Paul replied, "I am not ashamed to suffer as I do. Neither am I ashamed of my poverty. I have riches to which nothing in this life can compare."

Q: How do you make a living?

P: I really do make tents when I need money. But I rarely need money. Truly, as it is written, "the righteous live by faith."

Q: Whatever do you mean? One cannot *eat* faith, so faith cannot sustain life.

P: I suppose it depends on how one defines "life."

Q: Do you really expect me to engage in disputation regarding this Jewish superstition?

"Señor Fabius" . . . "Please, call me Marcus."

No need to be formal, I guess. And, on second thought, he decided, a little dialectic would be more interesting than general conversation. Quintilian was never good at making "chit-chat."

P: Very well, Marcus, would you not agree that, just because someone is wise, that does not mean he is therefore, good?

Q: Well, having studied under one of the wisest men in Rome, who was not known for virtuous character, I would have to agree!

P: Thank you. And wouldn't it be also the case that, in the contrary instance, one could be virtuous, but not wise?"[1]

"That brings to mind one of my classmates at Afer's school! He was indeed . . . "

"Oh, that's right!" Paul interrupted. "I had forgotten. You studied in Rome under Domitius Afer! What was that like?" "He taught me a *great* deal. Did you notice my method in the exordium today?" "That you juxtaposed the witness testimony with your own interpretation of the facts?" "Precisely! Afer." "I imagine the techniques you learned in Rome give you quite an advantage here in Hispania?" Quintilian grinned. "Absolutely, they do. My opponents rarely have the wherewithal to muster quantities of counter arguments sufficient to overcome such an onslaught. That's what he called this strategy, in fact: 'The Onslaught of Doubt.' He taught us to establish doubt through something he calls 'cross-examination.'" "Heh. 'Cross-examination.' Paul thought to himself. "I *like* the sound of that. I'll have to remember that one!"

---

1. The reader will have noticed by now a change in formatting. Dialectic, or "*disputatio*," is a form of inquiry, based on question and answer, exemplified in the famed "Socratic Method" of Plato's dialogues. Engaging in this familiar form, or style of discussion, would have been second nature for Hellenes. They picked up the habit in school. (There are worse habits one could pick up in school!) So we have here an instance of Paul and Quintilian sliding, effortlessly, between general discussion and dialectical inquiry. These elements will be handled thus throughout the book. This is my attempt at illustrating the differences between ordinary dialogue and the more technical and formal style of a dialectical disputation. As a result, some passages are rendered as Platonic dialogue, some in conventional prose, and some dialogue is designed to represent the dynamic of a rapid-fire exchange.

"Wha—" Quintilian did not understand the smile. Had he said something funny? "Nothing." It would not be worth the explaining. "Well, who else has influenced you? I must say, I find your style, and your deportment, enchanting!" Paul had decided to flatter the "child prodigy of Calagurris" in order to prepare the soil of his heart for the good seed of God's Word. As the maxim goes, "The way to a vain man's heart is through his vanity." "Thank you. You are more than kind. You know both my father, and his father, were rhetoricians?" "Really? Fascinating. So, rhetoric runs in your family." "Yes, I suppose you could say so. Julius Africanus certainly was the most vigorous speaker in the Hispania Tarraconensis of my youth, even more so than Afer." "Hmmm. I don't recall studying Africanus." "Looking back, I think him a bit too careful in his word choice, yet, ironically, too long-winded; given to excessive use of metaphors." "That *is* ironic." Paul was enjoying this discussion a great deal. He rarely got to recall his Hellenic studies.

"And of course, there was the time my grandfather took my father to hear Portius Latro when he held forth at the inaugural festivities at the Praetorium in Caesaraugusta. Grandfather always considered him the perfect orator: spoke of his fluidity of both motion and diction, as well as his mastery of the flowers of rhetoric. Said he was never affectatious, that his figures always served the larger purposes of his substantive points." A point of commonality! Paul was excited. "I studied that *very address*, 'On the Dedication of the Praetorium'! I must concur with your grandfather's opinion of Latro. Masterful. Moving. A rare talent. Not showy, like some."

"Ugh. In a word: Julius Secundus! Oh, I suppose I should be more kind to my good friend, but alas, I am afraid ol' Secundus is more concerned with style than with matter!" Paul cackled at this, then asked, straightway, "What is your opinion of Seneca the Younger? What do you make of his rhetorical doctrine?" "Typical of the Stoics, I suppose." He scratched his chin and consulted his memory, and wondered if he was being tested. "Nothing really original as I recall. His style was . . . especially pointed. Very little embellishment." "Oh. I see." Paul was hoping for some sort of endorsement. He admired Seneca's sober prose. "Pity, what happened to him."

Quintilian shot Paul a foreboding glance. "Yes. Pity. But we don't talk about him around here."[2]

---

2. Seneca the Younger was made to commit suicide in A.D. 65.

"Oh, sorry." Paul should have been a little more sensitive to their surroundings. "Well, tell me more about Afer's school. How was his teaching? His pedagogy? His curriculum?"

"Very typical Roman school of rhetoric; intense studies, with regular, highly competitive competitions and debates. I am a competitor, by temperament, but, oh my, how the pupils at Afer's school competed for accolades and glory!" Paul made a mental note regarding the combined influences of Quintilian's natural temperament, his upbringing, and his schooling.

"That explains the ambitions!" "Oh, yes! I have had a desire for fame as long as I can remember! I want to do *mighty* exploits! Men of my pedigree must never be content with the commonplace. Afer fed that desire, undoubtedly." "And your father and grandfather?" "Of course."

He could not help but note how, when Quintilian spoke those words, his tone, his pitch and demeanor, even his posture, all modulated, involuntarily. He sounded as though he were repeating a nostrum that had been grafted into his inmost being, through long hours of drill. Paul could exploit this . . . later, once the soil was ready; "tilled a bit more."

Quintilian surprised Paul by inviting him to continue the discussion, outside, "where there were fewer prying eyes"; more covering noise. Quintilian was eager to hear news from Rome, but the particular questions he had were of a delicate nature, so, when they were outside, a safe distance from the entrance, he put a few direct questions to the traveler.

"Which party were you in line to lead?"

"Party?"

"Pharisee or Saducee?"

"Well, neither, the only followers I lead are followers of Christ."

"Your background? Don't be coy with me, sir. I have important business inside."

"Ah, well, as I said, I was born into a household devoted to Pharisaism."

"So, you support the Zealots?"

"Excuse me?"

"Are you a supporter of the Jewish Revolt? Yes or no?"

"Well that is a complex matter, I'm not sure a simple 'yes' or 'no' . . ."

"Nonetheless, I need to know with whom I am engaged; whether we can even continue this discussion, or if I should walk away now. I'm half inclined to walk away, at any rate. Your flattery belies your intentions. I am not easily vanquished, good sir."

Paul took this in stride.

"Well, as I said, I follow Christ and he taught his followers to "render unto Caesar the things that are Caesar's," so. . . ."

"What does *that* mean?"

"He was teaching his followers to observe the laws of man's kingdom, but also, of God's kingdom."

"This is preposterous. There is only one kingdom: The Roman Empire. All allegiance is due only to Caesar."

"But, Señor, it is well known in Rome that you have aligned yourself with Galba. Is that not evidence of, at least, divided allegiances?"

Quintilian was visibly rattled by Paul's reply. He did not like feeling that exposed.

"I will not get into a political discussion with you beyond the single question: Do you or do you not support the Jewish Revolt?"

"In a word, no."

"But you are, or were, a Pharisee! I am under the impression that Pharisees support the revolt and Sadducees do not. I would feel much more comfortable consorting with a Jew if I knew he were of the Sadducees."

"Well, Quintilian, I am afraid that is a sweeping generalization. The actual situation, as I say, is much more complicated. Opinions are divided."

"What of *yours*?"

"As a matter of fact, I am writing a letter to my kinsmen that will, in part, urge them to not join with the Zealots, that followers of Christ are misguided if they seek political solutions to what are, by and large, spiritual problems."

His concerns somewhat eased, Quintilian detected a note of doubt in the man's tone. He dropped the inquisition; took a more conciliatory tone. "You don't seem confident. Do you think you will have no influence on them?" "I don't know," replied Paul, in all candor, "if they'll even read it. I am actually unsure whether I should even put my name to it." "Why on earth?"

Without exchanging a word about it, the two men drifted toward the café across the street and sat down at the table at which we had met Maximus, Prosperus, and Probus. Quintilian ordered Mauritanian tea for them both, and sliced fruit to share, then continued.

"Although I myself am in no wise interested in your sect," Quintilian wished to be perfectly clear on that point, "I find it fascinating that you have managed to grow to the extent you have. These so-called 'Christians' seem to be everywhere and yet you are everywhere persecuted. I know Rome is utterly crawling with them! How have you all managed to sustain such growth over *three decades*? It is an unparalleled achievement, in my experience." "Well, of course the appropriate response is that God has been spreading his word of salvation to the ends of the earth, despite the wicked schemes of wicked rulers!" "Yes. Yes, of course. I could have predicted that response. But, I am asking a different sort of question. What are your organizing principles?" "I travel nearly all the time. The only time I am not on the road, in fact, is when I stop long enough to earn money for the next trip." Quintilian had naturally assumed a "Hebrew of Hebrews" would have had personal wealth. "You have to earn money? Have you no patrons? How much do you charge for your teaching?" "Nothing! It is free, so that no man may accuse us of profiting from the message we preach. I could have patrons, but I think it better that the Believers have a chance to support the work. Otherwise, they spend all the wealth God gives on their own appetites." "Interesting. *That*, I would *not* have predicted."

"When I work in a town, I stay there, with new converts, until the teaching begins to take root. After a reasonable amount of time has been devoted to establishing the 'saints,' as we are called, building them up in knowledge and understanding of The Way, leaders are chosen. These leaders are charged, before the Almighty, with tending the congregation, preaching the Word, and administering alms. If need be, some of my fellows are appointed to administer the congregation until such time that they can stand on their own." Paul hoped that the strategy would intrigue Quintilian as much as he himself had been intrigued by Quintilian's "cross-examination." He prayed under his breath that Quintilian would be the cornerstone of the new church in Hispania Tarraconensis. "Lord, let it be so." "And how long does this take?" Yes, this young man clearly had the gift of administration. Perhaps this is God's purpose. . . .

"Of course, we are working with people, who are flawed. It depends on the character and temper of the peoples in a given province. The men of Antioch and Galatia are quite reasonable fellows. Corinth, on the other hand . . . well," catching himself, "I do not wish to be unkind." "Ha! I have heard!" Quintilian made a gesture that suggested Corinthians were excitable. Then he looked his guest over and said, knowingly, "so now you will find out about the inhabitants of Hispania." Paul winked his reply, trying to be coy, and shifted the focus of the discussion. "Having established churches all over the world, from Jerusalem and Judea, now, even to the ends of the earth, I travel from time to time, to visit churches I have planted in various places, to see what sort of fruit they have borne, so to speak. And, in between visits, I write letters that they circulate, for their edification and instruction. That is how I organize my efforts; tend my fields, so to speak. "Mmmm . . ." Quintilian was starting to lose interest.

"More tea?" The waiter had finally checked on them. "Yes, please." Paul sensed waning interest, so he decided an illustration would help. "For example," he pulled the manuscript from the satchel resting on the floor at his side, "I am just now laboring over this treatise to my kinsmen, which will likely be distributed after my death at the hand of Nero." "What? How do you know you will die by Nero's hand?" "The course of events leads to that conclusion. It is inevitable, and I was made perfectly aware, when I left to come here, that, upon my return, sentencing and execution would be swift."

"No more appeals?"

"Perhaps. I'm not really sure. As God wills. . . ."

"I will be in Rome soon. Perhaps I can help?"

"Thank you. You are kind to offer. I haven't money sufficient for. . . ."

Paul trailed off, supposing Quintilian is too often asked to supply his services gratis. Paul did not wish to be beholden to a nonbeliever for legal representation. Zenas had served him so well. Neither did he wish to disclose too much his opinions about Nero to an officer of the Roman courts. That would turn out good for neither of them. "I will cross that bridge when I come to it. For now, I long to travel to the end of the earth . . . to Brigantium."

Quintilian's clerk, Maximus, caught his eye from across the way. He was motioning that court was about to reconvene. "Well, at any rate, I'm glad that unpleasantness is nearly concluded. Such a pity we cannot live lives of peace and prosperity. Perhaps Fortune will shine on us all, very soon " . . . Quintilian trails off; he is circumspect.

"This is ever my prayer," Paul replied, understanding . . . but not fully. "Other than the revolt, I personally believe things are better by the day. We have new roads, new colonies are prospering across the realm, weather is improving, so we will soon have plenty to eat, new trade routes are opening up between Samothrace and lands to the East. If only something could be done about Nero." Paul froze. There it was. He glanced around to see if anyone was within earshot. All the surrounding tables were empty. Was it a test? He pretended it had never been uttered. "But all these are physical and material goods. How are we doing *spiritually*?"

Shocked at his sudden indiscretion, and glad it had not been answered in kind, Quintilian stood up and asked, feigning interest, "Material good, spiritual good? What's the difference?"

P: I thought we had established that one can be rich in things but poor in virtue?

Q: Certainly. But surely material blessings come to us as a reward for virtuous living? So they are two sides of the same coin.

Where was that confounded waiter? Quintilian looked around the place. He hasn't been out in some time and we're the only. . . . "There you are!" Quintilian says, accentuating "there," to communicate his displeasure with the waiter's tardiness, pointing at the cups to indicate they needed more tea.

P: Is it not true that the fruit of possessing a good spirit is happiness?

Q: Yes, O Socrates.

P: Bear with me, now.

Q: But, will I be happy doing so? Heh, heh.

Quintilian was pleased with himself.

P: And happiness, as Socrates determined, is the highest good, the summum bonum, for man?

Q: I would not dispute this.

P: And a great accumulation of material goods does not make one happy?

Q: I've known too many wealthy men. No. In fact, many men must find happiness apart from their material goods.

P: Thank you for that. So, happiness is a good in itself, and happiness is the fruit of the life lived well, but, material goods do not produce happiness, therefore, spiritual goods and material goods are not essentially the same.

Q: That is a clever bit of *disputatio*, but it doesn't really get to the root of things, now does it?

P: True. It was formally elegant, I suppose, but, ultimately, it does miss the mark.

Q: Look, just tell me what your religion teaches! Be clear. Be concise. What is its essence?

Quintilian took a long, easy draft of the sweet tea, self-satisfied at having taken control.

P: To sacrifice for the other, serving and giving, expecting nothing in return. This example we learn from our master.

Q: But I thought you said, only minutes ago, that mankind is inherently evil; that he is selfish? This makes no sense.

P: Not only the example, but the very power, the desire to give, unselfishly, comes from God.

Q: I must disagree. I believe what most pleases the gods is to do great deeds for the betterment of the demos. This is one's duty, and yes, I have faith that the fates reward those who do good for others with spiritual blessings. So my religion teaches that I should *expect* good fortune when I am mindful to do my duty to do good. I will to do good to others.

P: You say your heart desires to do good, and well you should. It is right to feel pity for the poor, filthy beggar on the side of the road (or at the back of the prætorium).

Quintilian chuckled.

P: If you felt nothing, I would worry about you! But the heart is also, as the scripture clearly says, 'full of all sorts of wickedness,' is it not?"

Quintilian balked a little at the simplification, but he acquiesced. The unease he felt with such talk, here in public, mounted.

P: Well, at any rate, you said you are familiar with my letter to the Roman Christians. Do you recall a brief discursus—not much amplified, but still rather stylized—on man's need for redemption?

Q: No, but I just don't see where religion offers more than exhortations to keep the law, to do good works, and the reward one can expect for pleasing the gods? There is no more. To do good to one's neighbor is the fulfillment of the law!

Catching himself, he lowered his voice to a whisper, leaned closer, tapping his index finger on the table for emphasis, "Doing good for one's neighbor is the fulfillment of the law."

P: On the contrary, my friend. According to my doctrine, Faith comes from God alone; our only duty is to believe on His Son, and that very belief is a gift of the Spirit. Certainly you agree that, if salvation is granted according to our efforts, it is no longer a gift, but a wage?

Q: What? The foolishness compounds . . .

P: (Ignoring him) As I quoted from Torah, in my letter to the Roman Christians,

> *all have sinned and fall short of the glory of God. None is righteous, no, not one.*

Quintilian's piety was under assault. His heart now pounded, he was flush, and he wished, mightily, that the judge would reconvene. Where was Maximus? "I don't believe that. I am not a bad person. I am so much better than most of the people I know. I give of all I have! I care for the poor! I serve the state, always striving to make the world a better place. And I am happy to do so!" A torrent of self-justification oozed from his fractured vanity.

Paul simply nodded and lay some coppers on the table, enough to cover the refreshments and a little extra. They both got up and headed across the street toward the Provincial Court. Just then, Zenas and I walked up. Paul asked us to find a suitable space for our evening session and suggested we take something to eat, and said he would follow as soon as he and Quintilian finished up. Apparently, they were in the middle of something intense. Quintilian was very silent; somewhat flushed.

"Were you able to get us good rooms?" "Yes, Sir," says I. "One denarii each. We are just down the hall from the girls and their brother. They will all be here this evening!" The rooms were well kept, by a Christian family. "Wonderful!" Paul saw God's hand in our having met "the children" right away. But more than that, he thought the meeting with Quintilian was providential. He had an uncommon capacity for leadership. I didn't really see that in him, but Zenas seemed to think he could get to him through his clerk, Maximus. Again, we shall see. We sat at the table they had just vacated. The patio was filling up. Paul and Quintilian crossed the street and disappeared into the crowd gathering around the court. Zenas watched after them. He had wanted Paul to introduce him to the great lawyer, but it was not to be. Maybe later.

"You started to show me your manuscript, there in your satchel, but we took a different path. Tell me about your new letter!" Paul was not the only one who could control the conversation by resorting to flattery. He patted the scroll for emphasis, through the rough-woven fabric. "Thus far it is only a draft in my mind, but I think I would like to employ a number of maritime metaphors to illustrate spiritual truths; that Israel set sail under rough seas, which represents the old covenant, but now the winds have shifted, and the fair winds of the new covenant have taken them to happier shores. Something along those lines."

Quintilian looked around. Maximus was nowhere. He was supposed to come fetch me. Hope I'm not late. He continued, struggling to pay attention. "That's, er, fanciful." "Well, I'm still working on it." Paul disliked discussing his work before it was ready for publication. "And, how long ago did you say you wrote to the Roman Christians? Seems to me it was only lately circulated." "It has been nearly five years now." Paul was surely surprised that Quintilian knew so much about his latest letter.

"I would think you would wait a little longer before releasing another letter?" "Why would it be too soon? I want to get the word out." "It seems you have a very heavy emphasis, and I don't mean to offend, perhaps too heavy, on the written word. I should think your message would lose some of its power if your primary vehicle for disseminating it is the written word? The pure, spoken word is manifestly more powerful for refreshing the well-springs of a community, is it not?" "Quintilian, who is playing Socrates now?" They both had a good laugh at Paul's thrust. "Notions like these are what drove me to seek you out! I rarely have occasion to explore these matters! And I agree with you entirely! The spoken word *is* powerful! But, in truth, they are all so connected, so inseparably linked with one another, that if any one of them is neglected, we labor in vain at the other two. It is my hope, nay, I instruct my elders, that these letters be read aloud, studied closely, which is to say, read silently, expounded upon, and I presume, in the schools, at least, written about. So, one would expect, the combined effect of all three modes to be superior to the spoken word only."

"One method I find satisfactory, when it comes to educating my apprentices, is the *suasoriae*, speeches of advice to historical figures. By having them give advice to Socrates, say, at critical junctures in his trial, they work on both writing and speaking persuasively, not to mention learning a little bit about jurisprudence." "That sounds like a great exercise. Sound pedagogy." "In fact, they exercise their prowess in reading inwardly, as well, by virtue of their having to understand the *Trial of Socrates* and any other cases that apply." Quintilian's parry was impressive! "This is true."

Paul truly admired Quintilian's modern perspective. He, himself, sought to spread the gospel by whatever means possible. And, yes, the interplay, and congruence, between speech, writing, and reading, was of prime importance when it came to educating the young. "I preface my exercise by establishing poor Socrates's need to employ lines of argument less offensive to his auditors!! They have such fun with it and learn so much! Say! Why not do something of that nature in your letter there?" Truth be told, Quintilian wasn't too keen on the maritime motif.

"Hmmm . . . " Paul considered the idea, but only for a brief moment. "I think I would be more inclined to include controversiae than suasoriae. There are falsehoods plaguing churches; falsehoods of many kinds. And I would prefer to focus on explicating truth rather than, as illuminating as it may be, dealing in speculation. Sophia, contemplation of first principles, is the highest kind of knowledge." "I find this rather amusing, coming from a Christian teacher. Your entire religion is based on speculation!" "But my point is," Paul made a strategic dodge. There would be time for eristic later! "My point is that I want my letters always to be didactic, because my aim is to communicate Christian truth, not the cultivation of rhetorical skills, or even the splitting of theological hairs." Quintilian thought to himself, "Ha. Silly Christians. They are weaving an entire tapestry of mythos, whole cloth. Fiction upon fiction. Ah, but one must not give offense . . . ")

"I sacrifice all to bring the Good News to these people. When I bring the message of hope, I cast it up in figures. But when it comes to establishing them in the faith and growth in knowledge of spiritual matters, I do not want them to get the impression I am playing with words, or worse yet, that I am smitten with my own fancy; my powers of invention." "Ha! This much is clear!" Quintilian looked his guest over and said, in summation, "so now I know why you've come all the way to Hispania." Paul winked his reply, trying to be coy.

"Having established churches all over the world, from Jerusalem and Judea, now, even to the ends of the earth, from time to time, I travel to visit the churches I planted hither and yon, to see what sort of fruit they bore, so to speak. I prune them, cultivate, and nurture. And, in between visits, I write letters that they circulate, that they may grow."

"Mmmm . . . " Quintilian was fast losing interest.

Quintilian wants terribly to walk away and get back to his work, but something about this strange little man is quite fetching. He was one of the most interesting and learned men he had ever met. Maximus appeared in the doorway, motioning to his master.

"I can think of no other more important topics of discussion, my friend, Paul. We have initiated a number of interesting and important lines of inquiry. I have much more to say; more veins to be mined; more to learn. But, I must now go attend to this Sabinus business, then tomorrow, after sentencing, I am off to my family's villa, outside Calagurris, to rest for a week and prepare for a lengthy sojourn, out of country. And I have business in Caesaraugusta, on the way, that should take half a day. Would you accompany me?"

"I'm sorry, I have only a few weeks for business across Hispania, then it's back to Rome."

"No, I meant at my family's villa in Calagurris!"

"Wouldn't it be politically unwise for you to be consorting with me? Where is Calagurris?"

"I suppose so, but we can be discrete. Calagurris is up the Iberus River Road, four days from Caesaraugusta, in La Rioja."

"I don't think I have time for that. We will go through Caesaraugusta, but Brigantium is. . . ."

"If you come with me, I will see to it that you get to Brigantium! The villa is not entirely out of the way. We'll have lots of time to talk on the road, then you can rest for a couple of days, up at my place. You will be smitten with its beauty! Then go to the coast. Meet me in five days, at sunrise, under the 'Temple Rock' on the Iberus River Road to Calagurris one half mile north of the first marker out of Caesaraugusta. Come with me. We will work on your manuscript, together! It will be your finest work!"

Quintilian's insistence confirmed Paul's sense that God was at work in this young "prodigy's" heart. That was it, then. Plans change.

P: There is a very good chance you will find me, along with my traveling companions, waiting for you when and where you suggest. I am not at liberty to say for sure that such will be the case. I do not know which way the wind will blow, if you catch my drift, but, unless God intervenes, I can certainly accomplish my aim here, this evening, then finish up on our return.

Q: Splendid! We will resume this conversation when it is just we four. Until then . . .

P: God be with you.

Q: Fare thee well.

If he had realized what was taking place, not half a mile from where he stood, the young man with the filthy tunic and weariness and anxiety written all over his sunburned face, would have rushed ahead to intercept his friends. But he was too hungry to continue. He stopped to eat breakfast. He was on the verge of panic, but he tried to contain himself long enough to ask a few questions, "Where would I look for them in Caesaraugusta?" "Well," replied Maximus, "Our master is finishing up a few final details on some legal issues with the Praetor, but . . . " "So I should—" his apprehensions got the best of him. Undaunted by the young man's lack of manners, Maximus finished his conjecture: " . . . but the sort of business he has in Caesaraugusta could take him from one end of the city to the other. I should think it would be very difficult to catch them there." The young man slammed the table with his fist and swore. He had barely slept in two days; barely eaten. Sensing this, Maximus overlooked the outburst and, instead, handed the lad an apple from the bowl behind him. Blushing, he thanked him much. While he ate, Maximus advised, "Here is what I would do. We know they're headed to Calagurris. There is but one road from Caesaraugusta to Calagurris, up the Iberus. They'll be in Caesaraugusta no more than 24 hours. I would wait at the place where that road leaves Caesaraugusta and you will surely see your friends, probably early that morning would be my guess. Or, you could go with me when I leave in two hours." He thanked him, asked directions to the nearest livery, turned on his heel and was off to hire a horse. He hoped to overtake them on the road this very day.

As he was about to trot away, Probus emerged from the Praetorium. Maximus explained the young traveler's situation, at which Probus remarked, "You are in luck!" The young man stopped dead in his tracks. "I happen to know the girls and their brother have arranged to meet those gentlemen at the marketplace in Caesaraugusta four days hence, precisely at noon. Apparently they intend to hold public meetings. . . ."

"Girls? Brother?" He was in the dark, but he hadn't much time to spare. He would get caught up on all that had transpired when he found them in the market square of Caesaraugusta. "Six bells. I will be there." He raised his hand in thanks, but never turned around. He was pleased. As he walked toward the café, he smiled for the first time in days. Finally, some good news! Time to eat.

9

Clement Catches Up

"WELL," DECLARED POLYXENE, WIDE were her eyes, deep her appreciation. The truths Paul taught filled her with life so that she exuded a spiritual radiance which compounded her natural beauty, "I thought it lovely, profound, and uplifting." "Thank you, my child. You are too kind." Paul sincerely appreciated her kind words, but remained unconvinced. "I just wish I had had another half-hour with them." Paul always wanted another half-hour! Truth be told, he was too exhausted by the journey from Tarraco to Caesaraugusta to teach with his usual vigor. He could barely string together a coherent sentence. Paul remarked, of Xanthippe and Polyxene, "These two have a zeal that reminds me of Basilissa and Anastasia!"[1] I nodded agreement. Zenas was a few feet away, sheltered from the early afternoon heat, fanning himself and explaining the homily to Maximus, Xanthippe, Diocles, and Prosperus. Paul tended to operate on the extreme deep end of the pool; Zenas had become adept at "pre-digesting" Paul's messages for the uninitiated; "throwing them a lifeline," so to speak. Sometimes he felt like a mother sparrow feeding her children! But Maximus and Diocles were not all that hungry, so they went looking for an open table, in the shade. Xanthippe and Prosperus, on the other hand, pelted Zenas with questions. After a few earnest attempts, he turned to Paul for help. "Brother Paul, these two need to understand more fully your point about 'not being justified by works of the law.' Paul was, of

---

1. Sisters, martyrs in Rome who buried the bodies of Christians tortured to death under Nero. They themselves were tortured, refused to forsake the faith, and were beheaded, perhaps even during the time Paul and company were evangelizing Hispania. He may or may not have known of their demise at the time of this comparison. (Also from Meinardus, "Paul's Missionary Trip to Spain.")

course, happy to oblige. Regardless of whether Zenas could handle their questions, which he could, it was good for these youngsters to learn directly from the Master (and it renewed Paul's vitality, as well).

Paul didn't even notice the road-worn visage walking gingerly in his direction, anxious, exhausted, starving and covered with highway dust, head-to-toe. Under his cap, beneath light brown, stringy shoulder-length locks, toting some sort of rucksack, I recognized Brother Clement of Rome. "So," I thought it best to temper with a modicum of levity Clement's obviously frazzled state. "Nice of you to join us, Brother Clement!" He was *not* amused.

"Wha-?" Paul wheeled around, eyes fixed on the bedraggled novice. "Well, well, well. What aspect of 'first light' did you not understand, Clement?" barked Paul, clearing his throat (to keep from laughing. There was no obstruction). Clement *was* a sight! He could not maintain eye contact. Staring off to his left, taking a deep breath, he explained, trembling, how he'd missed the boat, and how, by God's grace, he had made passage the very next day. "Young man," I said sternly, "do you know what an excuse is? It is the 'skin of a lie, stuffed with reason.'"

"Yes, sir. Sorry, sir." Turning to Paul, "Please forgive me my tardiness." Anger and exhaustion gave way to feelings of failure. But Brother Paul could contain his joy no longer, "Ah, Clement," hugging him warmly, "I am so thankful God sent his holy angel before you, to protect you from all harm and danger, and now you are with us. That is what matters." Clement patted him on the shoulder in agreement, and wept a little. It had been a difficult nine days, and now he could relax in the company of his mentor and fathers in the faith. His emotional release was short lived. I handed him two pieces of fruit, a loaf, and a skin of water.

"You realize, young man, only this morning we were trying to figure out how to get word to the team up in Gaul whom we were to connect with in Burdigala? That they need to be made aware of our change of plan?" "Who? Team?" His mouth was so full we barely understood him. He washed down the mouthful with a gulp from the skin. "Who is traveling with the two of you?" "Luke?" Paul wanted me to get Clement caught up while he resumed his private lesson for the girls and Prosperus.

"Zenas is with the two of us."

"Are there nine total, then?"

"No, ten. We brought along Apollos in your stead."

"Apollos, eh?"

He dared not give voice to the thought that amused him upon hearing they had taken along Apollos. I could tell what he was thinking, made eye contact, and shook my head, in a silent exhortation to mind his tongue; to not provoke Brother Paul. "We split into three teams, one heading north into Gaul, one heading South, along the coast, to Nova Carthago on the Via Herculea, and our team, 'Team Beta.' We were on our way to Brigantium, up the Via Domitii, but there has been a change of plans, so we will rejoin Team Alpha, from Burdigala in Gaul, here in Caesaraugusta, upon our return from Calagguris."

"Oh, so just the three of you, then? Wait? Calagguris? I thought the plan was to meet on the Western Shore, at, at . . . up the Via Aquitania?"

"Burdigala."

"Yes, but . . . "

"Ah. Right. Change of plans . . . "

"Yes. On the second day of our voyage across to Tarraco we held a very fruitful strategy session and decided we would split into three groups and cover as much of Hispania Tarraconensis and Southern Gaul as possible, in 20 days."

"I see. Good plan. Good roads. So, why the change?"

"To make a long tale more brief, Paul made the acquaintance of Marcus Fabius Quintilianus in the Provincial Court at the Forum in Tarraco."

"*The* Quintilian?"

"Yes, *The* Quintilian. There is some sort of affinity between them, which Paul views as a sign from God. He hopes to convert him."

"Oh, my . . . "

" . . . so decided it was worth a change of plan to accept his invitation to the family villa in Calagguris. We are to spend two days there and then we aim to go all the way to Brigantium!"

Clement beamed at the prospect of an unexpected adventure. "I have always dreamt of visiting Cala—"

I said nothing; simply shook my head, side-to-side, slowly, and grinned. "Ugh. I'm not going, am I?" Clement, ever the optimist, had recognized an opportunity to redeem himself. Paul broke off his own conversation and answered, "You shall have an adventure, alright, my delinquent friend! You are to go to Burdigala, post haste."

"Well, it's decided then," said Zenas, walking over to rejoin us after having spent the last several minutes talking with the others, around their table, in what appeared to be a fairly intense planning meeting. "I shant be accompanying you tomorrow, I'm afraid." This was a sudden development. "Diocles just informed me that, Xanthippe had, quite forcefully, apparently, suggested that they delay their departure for Toletum by another day so that we can spend a little more time discussing the teachings of Jesus. He assented!" Polyxene bolted to her sister and gave her a great bear hug! "Maximus learned, only an hour ago, that Probus is on his way, from Tarraco." Zenas made a showy, dramatic, wink of the eye. Xanthippe blushed; Polyxene giggled; Diocles frowned. (Apparently there was more at play here than passion for God's Word.) "Prosperus has business here in Caesaraugusta that will take several days, as well. As you can see, God has provided exceeding abundantly right here in Caesaraugusta, so I think I will stay put, if it's all the same. They should be ready to "get wet" when you return!"

Who could argue with such a God-ordained plan? So, Zenas stayed in Caesaraugusta to work the vineyard of the Lord amongst Quintilian's clerk, Maximus, and the Christian lad, Prosperus, and of course, Xanthippe and Polyxene and Diocles! Clement took a day to refresh himself and hire the fastest horse in town, then took off to intercept Team Alpha, up in Burdigala. They were instructed to depart immediately upon his arrival and meet in the marketplace at Caesaraugusta on Day Twenty, so we could travel together back to Taracco. They would discuss plans for establishing elders and deacons in strategic locations along the road so that, before our return to Rome, once we heard from Team Gamma, we would have a "master plan" for establishing churches throughout Hispania and Gaul the next two to five years. Word was circulated amongst believers that we would baptize and commission leaders in Caesaraugusta on Day Twenty and Taracco on Day 25. The other teams were to teach only, then baptize and commission upon their return, after we departed for Rome. (As it turned out, there was a notable exception in Gaul. Apollos and Barnabas found that the Words of Life had already taken root extensively among a small enclave of one hundred souls of Aquitania, who had settled the Garumna River valley, halfway between Tolosa and Burdigala. These lambs lived among wolves, practitioners of rank idolatry, so the brethren confirmed them in the faith, baptized them on the spot, even celebrated with them the Lord's Supper.)

10

Wisdom and Eloquence

THE PARTY MET, AS planned, at "Temple Rock," a prominent granite out-cropping that stood watch over travelers on the Rio Iberus Road. As they waited for all to be prepared, Quintilian and Paul, as was swiftly becoming their habit, engaged in conversation, regarding some bit of news from Rome, about state funded education or the like. Paul pondered, for some time, as he looked Quintilian over, whether or not it would be worth the asking. He smiled, inhaled slowly, and decided to risk it, "A friend came to visit me, just last week, and attributed to you a saying that I had hoped to discuss if we met when I came to Tarraco." "Oh, really? What did I say, now?" Quintilian laughed to himself. "He said he had attended a lecture of yours, on education of the young," Quintilian nodded, recollecting the occasion, "and that he was struck by an observation you made in passing, to the effect that, *'above all things the orator must study morality.'*" "Yes. Umhmm." "My question was, 'Whose morality?' Does it matter in what sort of morality a child is immersed? My sensibilities tell me, 'Yes,' but I'd love to hear your answer, O Learned One," Paul bowed his head low in feigned abeyance.

"Well, what did your friend say I said?" He honestly had forgotten the point, he admitted, it was but a passing remark. "That was the problem that led to my bringing it up now. When I pressed him, he thought you may have presupposed eudæmonism, but he said he only inferred this." "Your friend was too kind. He presumed a higher degree of sophistication than I intended. I think I was assuming a common-sense morality that may be best understood in terms of civility, respect, integrity, and the like. 'General morality,' let us call it."

Paul was puzzled, "so your proposition was that 'above all things the young orator must study etiquette'?" "Well, friend, I admit I don't have it all worked out yet, but you make it sound droll." "Oh, I'm sorry. I was simply attempting to formulate a proposition from which to launch a line of inquiry. I did not mean to give offence. Indeed, I wonder if this might not be the very conversation for which 'Fortune' has brought us together!"

P: Please allow me to make a new attempt: How do you define 'general morality'?

Q: Generally speaking, your friend was correct, I subscribe to eudæmonism.

P: Excellent! Aristotle's notion of the "good soul," associated as it is with the cultivation of personal virtue, provides many rules by which one may live life well."

Q: I agree.

P: But, from your talk, I surmise that you are interested in raising up men of good character to be civic leaders?

Q: That is important to me, yes. The alternative, ignoble leaders, can produce no end of unsavory consequences: corruption, tyranny, fraud, and, eventually, society breaks down.

P: Another emphasis, it seems to me, is your focus on industry and prosperity. Would it not be, in keeping with that aim, wise to complement "general morality" with the virtue of success?

Q: I'm not sure if you propose this seriously, but I think the virtue of honest labor is not to be underestimated. It involves, and will cultivate in the apprentice, integrity, loyalty, trust, and industry. It will make him, not only a leader, or a judge, or a lawgiver, but also, a diligent and fastidious worker and, eventually, artisan, master, and inventor.

P: Yes, and a strong community requires a strong foundation in commerce.

Q: This is well and good, my friend, but no, I am concerned about *actual* morality, virtue.

Paul smiled. This is what he hoped to hear.

P: Quintilian, you are wise beyond your years. Virtue is a good in itself.

Q: Seek first to be good, and to do good to your neighbor, and prosperity will follow. "Faith, Numina, Spirit."

P: Yes. I see a great deal of congruence between the position you espouse and Christian morality, with its focus on "service to neighbor."

Q: As do I. His head tilted slightly, his brow furrowed, and his eyes narrowed. Quintilian was growing suspicious.

P: I would offer a caveat, however.

Q: (with just a touch of sarcasm,) Pray, tell.

P: I find that the nature of the service, specifically, its motivation, makes all the difference.

Q: Of course. (Okay, I see where he is headed. Not the direction I anticipated. . . .) An examination of proper motives is always worthwhile!

P: Agreed. Service. Service that expects nothing in return, ought to form the basis for the morality at which you aim. I find especially egregious, some expectation of earning favor with God. Service, the aim of which is to become good or find favor with God, or with some other expedient in mind, personal gain, for example, is not a sufficient "primary good" on which to base a philosophy of virtue ethics.

This makes good sense to Quintilian. "I assent to, at least *prima facie*, the wisdom of your caveat, because that sort of sacrificial giving is the best material from which to build true community. Commerce is good, but kindness, generosity, and friendship provide strong pillars."

"Do you enjoy hunting? Fishing?" Paul did not know. "I've never had opportunity to do any of that. I did help bring in a large fish of some sort, up near Corinth. But I suppose you are talking about catching fish from the river?" "Indeed I am, and we have ponds and streams, as well" said Quintilian. "It is settled then. I will show you how it's done, we have a particular kind of fish, with long "whisker-like" protrusions. . . ." "Excuse me, Quintilian, I appreciate your enthusiasm," Paul felt the need to interrupt. Perhaps he couldn't accompany Quintilian after all. He seemed to have some big plans. " . . . but I'm afraid we must focus on the task at hand."

"Oh, well, if you need to get off . . . " Paul raised his hand, palm out. "No, no. I certainly appreciate your hospitality, it's just that I have only a few weeks to cover a lot of territory. I've been planning this trip for a long time. I look forward to our journey together, and to time at your villa—a couple days—but then we simply must be on our way to the coast." Quintilian was flexible. "Okay, then. I understand. As it says in the scroll of the book, 'Friend, let us make the most of each day for we know not what tomorrow will bring.'"

Our conversations ranged across myriad topics as we drove up the Rio Iberus. Two topics predominated: Rhetoric and ethics. We were riding along in silence when, unexpectedly, a horseman passed us, whipping his mount, giving us a start, and coaxing the animal to a full gallop. We followed him as, in a very brief moment, he disappeared around the corner, into the evergreens and shadows. All eyes were still glued to his dust trail when I seized my opportunity.

"Excuse me, Quintilian?" "Yes?" "Speaking of scrolls, what is this set, here in the elegant wood frame . . . is that olive?" "Yes, olive wood, embellished with ivory inlay and polished with resin!" "Now *that* is beautiful! Not to mention the beautiful contents!" "Good Doctor, you don't know the half! These scrolls contain knowledge on every subject proposed since the ancients. It is an "Encyclopedia; *Celsus's Encyclopedia.*" "Encyclopedia? Interesting. Impressive. How did you come by this storehouse of knowledge?" "It was a gift from Apronianus, partly in appreciation and partly in payment for my work on his behalf." "I see. Fortune has smiled on you!" He shot me a glance; he was surprised at my gesture of goodwill, acknowledging as I did his religion. "And I think God has blessed you," he winked, responding in kind. "Two of those scrolls are devoted to modern healing arts!" I reflexively took a shallow breath. "*Two* scrolls? On *medicine*? No!" "Yes!" "May I . . . " "Of course! Enjoy yourself."

Paul, not being at all satisfied with their initial exchanges, neither outside the Forum, nor on the road, was bold to make a procedural recommendation that, in theory, would enhance our discussions on the way to the villa. He proposed that we do, as a game, an extended dialectic on Truth, Beauty, and Goodness, to order our examination of the role of rhetoric in educating good men. (I opted out, preferring to focus my attention on the encyclopedia!)

The inquiry into the nature of beauty took an early, and predictable, turn: The beauty of nature. We were surrounded by God's majesty; enveloped in it. Hispania Tarraconensis is blessed with beautiful rivers, lush valleys, interesting rock formations, and farmland, neatly kept, rich in minerals, and all the bounty of plant and animal life. The countryside that raced past, and the mountains we skirted, all epitomized nature's beauty, with verdant cedars, elms, pines, myrtles, and olives.

An interesting line of talk emerged the second day of our journey up the Iberus. Somebody had mentioned something or other pertaining to Quintilian's trial, and Quintilian exclaimed, "Oh! That reminds me. You said, when we were standing outside the Forum, waiting for the trial to resume, that 'contemplation of first principles is the highest kind of knowledge.' I realize this is received wisdom, and, of course, Sophia is knowledge of the most grand, loftiest, of Truths. Nonetheless, I am just not so turned. I value *phronesis* above *sophia*!" Paul adjusted his position so he was more directly facing Quintilian than he had been, smiled and said, "Do tell . . . " Quintilian had apparently put a great deal of thought into this question, because his discourse lasted several miles.

Q: It seems to me that *phronesis*, practical wisdom, or prudence, insofar as it entails the application of first principles to wise judgment, is more useful, and to a greater extent, than is *sophia*. Sophia is beautiful, and she abides on a high and lofty plane, but, once we admire her beauty and elegance, what good is she? *Phronesis* comes down to where we live and helps us navigate the gray and murky waters of this plane, where things are not so clear, where the ground is a little more rough and uneven. Negotiating the rough byways of this life requires an instrument more subtle and more . . . more, I don't know. An instrument with more 'dexterity,' shall we say, than geometric or abstract reasoning.

"I am intrigued," Paul said, nodding. "Your point of view is novel, but makes perfect sense."

Quintilian was pleased with himself. He respected Paul. "I have been thinking along these lines for some time now. I see the dangers inherent in discounting *sophia*, but I remain unconvinced that it must necessarily be privileged over *phronesis* simply by virtue of its having to do with first principles. I think, when Aristotle identified the 'five intellectual virtues,' in his *Analytics* and his *Ethics*, he clearly discusses the virtues in terms of the "well-ordered mind," such that each virtue has its domain, and all are present in the 'well-ordered mind,' or 'well-turned soul,' available for treating of various kinds of questions, as they blossom in the life lived well."[1]

Paul and I both nodded in agreement. Neither of us found anything with which to disagree in what Quintilian had said. Phronesis is, after all, dependent upon knowledge of first principles for its proper function, so it does not forsake them. On the other hand, phronesis is of more use within the practical sphere than is sophia, where problem solving and making good decisions are concerned! These are fundamental to wise action, so, yes, Quintilian's point was well taken! One does not deduce, from a first principle, what needs to be done in a difficult situation, in life as lived. Not even the strictest of logicians operates in that fashion! This was an unexpected turn in our examination of Truth, and it helped us pass many an hour of what would have been otherwise, miles of monotony! Quintilian announced we had crossed into La Rioja; Calagurris was not much further.

Quintilian seemed quite interested in news from Rome; I could think of nothing but *Celsus's Encyclopedia.* I must admit, dear reader, that, for much of that journey, I slept. Or, at least, I tried to sleep. My constitution is not well disposed to such rapid travel. Paul and Quintilian were engrossed in conversation about matters for which I had little capacity and even less interest still, so the time flew by for those two! I did make an attempt to engage the driver, but he wasn't much for chit-chat. So I slept as much as I was able and looked forward to our arrival at the Fabius family villa. I would leave the boys to their talky talk. I had medical knowledge to acquire!

---

1. Aristotle wrote a number of works on reasoning, known collectively, as *The Organon* (Instrument). They have, throughout the Western tradition, been understood as an instrument to equip human beings for the life lived well. Aristotle begins with grammatical categories ("This is a noun, this is a verb . . . when combined in the following way these make a declarative statement. A declarative statement is a proposition. A proposition in doubt is a question," and so on.) He then examines (in his *Analytics*) analytical or demonstrative reasoning. This is the realm of syllogistic logic, of speculative reasoning, of absolutes. Then, in *The Topics*, and its companion volume, *On Sophistical Refutations*, he teaches dialectical reasoning. Dialectic operates in the contingent realm, where honest people can disagree; where opinions are divided. In the Hellenic curriculum (and therefore, in the classical liberal arts,) dialectic was taught in tandem with rhetoric, to equip young men and women of faith for lives of wise action, and to be eloquent leaders who serve both in the community and in hearth and home.

(For tips on teaching in tandem dialectic and rhetoric, to cultivate wisdom and eloquence, see: http://www.rhetoricring.com/practical-tips-for-teaching-rhetoric/)

Quintilian also seemed keenly interested in helping Paul with his writing. "Toward the middle of your letter to the Roman Christians," Quintilian noted, "you say something I find gripping. You write, that you . . . " Paul asked, "Oh, so you've read it?" "Yes I did. Finished it just before we left Tarraco, in fact. I bought a copy just after we met." "Bought a copy?" "I have friends in the business." Ha! Paul smiled and nodded his gratitude. "You write, in the letter to the Romans that you would forfeit your own soul for the sake of your kinsmen." "Indeed, I feel that way. I ache to see them accept God's salvation. The irony, that they were His 'Chosen People,' but they rejected Him, is too much to bear. So . . . yes." "Strong talk!" said Quintilian. "And yet, now, you are not even sure you can put your name on a letter in which you intend to share with them 'good news,' so called? I'm not sure I understand this devotion to people who, apparently, reject you, even on a personal level, at every turn?"

"Oh," Paul shook his head for emphasis, "believe me, I have given up on them many times. But, in the final analysis, I cannot. I love them. I say I am done with them, then, as we enter a new town, where do I go? The synagogue. I go to reason with them, cajole them, plead. I have become all things to all men that the more would be saved." "But, why?" Quintilian was stymied. "They do not have ears to hear what you have to say! Are you not 'chasing after wind'?" I had to smile. I was pretending to be asleep, just behind them, among the boxes, curled up on a pile of blankets and tack. Quintilian was very perceptive. "I cannot deny, they are a stiff-necked lot. And my calling is to the Gentiles. They are much easier to persuade, to be sure! But the Hebrews are my people. And they are God's people. The God of Abraham, Isaac, and Jacob has chosen them, so I cannot bear to think of their missing out on the coming of Messiah. I cannot bear it."

"Well, if you are going to write a letter to them, it is clear you will not be able to utilize the same strategies you utilize when writing to Greeks and Romans! These Hebrews, as you say, are a stubborn lot!" Paul only laughed. "You will need to write to their nature." "What?" Paul had no idea what he meant. "Breaking through that rough exterior will require strong figuration. You will need to pique the imagination, to stir the emotions, to soften their hearts of stone."

Quintilian was so insightful, so eloquent, when it came to moving the souls of his auditors, Paul was compelled to seek his counsel. So Paul disclosed that he had already decided to utilize a "promise motif," a stock element of his epistles, because he could envision Hebrews being "softened" as Quintilian put it, by the story of Sarah and Hagar. "It helps illustrate, like no other story, the problem of reliance on one's own works to fulfill God's designs. That 'His ways are not our ways,' so to speak." "Yes, yes," Quintilian replied, "But, as I recall, you already mined that vein, did you not? Do you think you could replace the, uh, the analogue of Haggai and Sarah to promise and works, uh, substitute that for some other theme?"

"I suppose I could . . ."

"This time, take a less familiar, more abstract, er, mystical tack."

"Perhaps something about sailing?"

"Yes, perhaps. But sailing is so mundane. It may provide a rich pool of analogies from which to draw, but I was thinking of something that will really *grip* them."

"Hmmm. I suppose the centrality of the Passover narrative would be the best, most powerful, most central, element of Hebrew faith one could utilize to 'grip' Hebrews."

"Good. Say on. . . ."

"Jesus as the 'Paschal Lamb.'"

"That sounds very straightforward. I was thinking something very cryptic or unusual would prepare them to better receive the didactic parts of your letter."

"Hmm. Okay. That makes good sense."

"What is the most strange and wonderful, even cryptic story in your holy writ?"

"Well, I suppose,"

Paul said, gazing at the horizon, scrolling though the storehouse of his biblical memory that would have to be when the sun . . . No! *Melchizedek*! Yes. Barely a mention. But different than anything else in the entire corpus! King of Salem he was. That would make him Prince of Peace. At the very least, he is a type of Christ Jesus, as well, and some speculate that he may have, in fact, been the Son of Man in a pre-incarnate manifestation." "Interesting." Quintilian was just being polite. "Well, be that as it may, do you believe this interpretation is commonly held amongst Jewish Christians? Or amongst the Jews, generally?" "Absolutely not. It is rather a new understanding. Some amongst the Judeans and Syrians have been developing it." Quintilian thought that sounded promising.

"Then why not exploit that novelty?! It would give your treatise distinction and make a contribution to the literature. It could certainly fuel a great deal of figuration. I could imagine a number of interesting parallels one could develop." "Mmmmm. . . . Yes. Thank you, Marcus. Thank you, indeed."

For some reason the word "Kairos" came to Paul. Yes, he thought, this seems like an opportune moment to plant a little more seed . . . "Marcus, you have wisdom beyond your years!" "Thank you. My whole life, thus far, has been devoted to the acquisition of wisdom, especially *practical* wisdom, precisely because it guides my attempts to serve my fellow man." "It shows in all you do. Thank you for sharing your wisdom with *me*!"

Quintilian actually choked up a little, but then tried to hide it from Paul. "Oh! Must've gotten a gnat in my eye." This young man obviously had a heart to help others, even those with whom he held significant disagreements. We were climbing a hill now, but there were no obstructions, so the going was steady. Paul had to hand it to these Romans. . . . "Do you sense some special connection between us, Marcus? Because I do." "Certainly. It is a rare joy to meet someone with whom you can discuss anything under the sun so freely, and on such a deep level." "My feelings exactly." Paul looked to make sure I was asleep, not wanting to give offence. He needn't have worried. I knew what he was up to. I was still not asleep, but I was praying, hard. "Our meeting, and this trip—never have I had such pleasant conversation, over such an extended period—they constitute what I call," Quintilian commiserated, "a 'magical moment'! I hope that doesn't sound too silly or effeminate." "No, not at all, friend. I brought this up because I feel the same way! I am much older than you, but I concur, rarely have I felt a more solid or deep connection, which developed in so short a period of time, with *any* man. And, if this trip is any indication, I can hardly wait until we get to Villa Fabianus!"

"Indeed!"

"This is God's doing, Marcus. It has to be."

"I count your friendship as a blessing, as well."

"There is a divine purpose for our finding one another, Marcus. I believe God is calling you unto himself."

Quintilian had anticipated this turn for some time. He said nothing, only thought to himself, "I thought I made it clear to this chap that I have big ambitions. I am not inclined to throw my life away as he has." Paul continued, "There is a passage, from the Eighth Proverb, that goes, 'Whomever finds wisdom finds life and obtains favor from the Lord, but he who hates wisdom loves death.' Marcus, I perceive in you a man of uncommon wisdom, and I believe you have obtained favor of the Lord." "How kind of you to say so." No words passed between the two for many miles.

Finally, we came to Rio Cidacos and turned North by Northeast, back toward the Iberus. As we hugged a stretch of heavily wooded hills that ran parallel to the road for some time, and were cooled by the long afternoon shadows, Paul broke the silence. "Marcus, You are so kind to entertain us. Thank you." "It is my great honor to have you both," came Quintilian's gracious reply. "I look forward to revisiting that exordium you gave the other day," Paul said. "That argument was both erudite and eloquent." "You exaggerate, Paul."

We had been climbing a hill for some time. While Quintilian sketched for me his closing argument from the trial of Naevius Apronianus we topped the hill, and the way down the other side was quite bumpy. And we were back in the afternoon sun. "Please, make yourself comfortable and hold on! We're only a half-hour away!" "Thank you," I was, in fact, holding on for my life, and as far as being comfortable, there was no chance of that. "The argument depended brilliantly on the presupposition that, that. . . . Oh, drat. I don't recall it at this time, but you used that particular presupposition, whatever it was, as the seat of your argument. It was a first rate strategy."

"Oh," said Quintilian, prompting me, "you mean the one about Sabinus drawing faulty inferences based on Naevius's physical appearance and various looks and actions?" "Indeed! That is it. Yes! Brilliant! By returning, rehearsing, and reiterating you built such strong doubt in the minds of those present, that Naevius was in no way motivated in the way Sabinus supposed he was, I suspect Sabinus himself doubted his own testimony by the time you finished!" "You really think so? I thought it a rather ordinary bit of argumentation."

Paul chimed in, "Granted, perhaps the appeals to imagination could have been a little more vivid, but the logic and the ethos were extraordinary!" "So kind of you to say. You are trained in rhetorical arts, then? Where did you study?" "In the Hellenic school of Tarsus, and, when I was ten I had the good fortune to study under Gamaliel in Jerusalem. I learned dialectic, rhetoric, Greek, and the new methods of handling aright the holy scriptures."

"Interesting."

"We studied The Torah and Talmud; Pentateuch, Prophets, and Psalms."

"Of course."

"But, in Christian doctrine, I had *no* teacher, save Jesus of Nazareth alone."

"Really? Wasn't he already out of the picture when you first came to Jerusalem?"

"Oh, you are familiar with these events?"

"Oh, I have watched these developments with more than a little interest. So, how is it that an already deceased rabbi taught you about the fulfillment of the Law and Prophets?"

"First, as you must be aware, since you are familiar, we contend that He is *not* dead." Quintilian nodded politely.

Just then, we crowned a hill and before us opened up the most lovely valley where, off in the distance near the dark and rocky foothills of the Seven Valleys, the Cidacos and Iberus joined. The plantation was a vision of lovely, symmetrical, industry and organization. The lanes leading up to the villa were all straight, well groomed, and tree-lined. The vineyard, focused on a hillside to the south, behind the villa, was neatly planted in meticulously placed rows of lush vines, propped up with crossed wood laths. Down on the bottoms, barley, wheat and oats were sprouting in arrow-straight furrows of rich brown earth. A number of stunning, immaculately groomed, chestnut horses, with long dark manes and tales, frolicked in a pasture near the stable to which we were headed. "We have arrived, gentlemen. Welcome to my family's estate, Calagurritanum!" He had the driver pause so we could take it in. A gentle breeze, rich with the fragrance of wildflowers, rustled the elm and myrtle leaves. We got out of the cart, walked a few feet onto a sandstone ledge, shadowed by a large cedar and took in the vast, verdant, beauty. Two parakeets warbled their ode to spring from a twig just above and behind us.

Paul broke the silence, though tentatively; respectfully. He said, in little more than a whisper, "Marcus, the question that captivated the Greeks, that captivated Plato, 'How shall we live our lives?' is answered for me now." Before us spread Calagurritanum, the epitome of beautifully ordered industry. Of course, Paul and Quintilian had to discuss what, precisely, made it so beautiful!

Paul mentioned the beauty of the layout, how well-planned was each division: orchard, vineyard, pasture, and grain field. "Thank you. Father put a lot of thought into this operation. Do you see, away over there?" He pointed across the valley, across the Iberus, toward the hillside, to some rocky ground with a rough road leading up to it. "We also have a mine and our own foundry across the way!" "Impressive," was all Paul could muster in reply. He was, simultaneously, interested by Quintilian's villa and, being raised in the city, could not relate. "Talk about beauty!" Quintilian had clearly just broached his favorite topic, other than rhetoric and ethics, of course. "Talk about beauty," he repeated himself for emphasis. "Consider the planting of fruit-trees: arranged as they are, in regular intervals. What is more beautiful than the well-known quin-cunx, which, in whatever direction you view it, presents straight lines?"[2] Indeed, Paul could not deny how pleasing it was to the eye. "But a regular arrangement of trees is advantageous also, because each then attracts an equal portion of the juices of the soil. You see?" "So it is good for growth? And they produce more fruit?" Paul asked. "Indeed, they do. I keep records and compare with neighbors who don't practice these modern, scientific methods. Results do not lie!"

"Notice also," he now directed our gaze toward the olive grove, "the tops of my olive, I trim with my knife every time they grow too high, which causes them to spread more gracefully in a round form and, at the same time, also produces more fruit because there are more branches! Form and function! Beauty *and* prosperity!" I admired the amount of thought he had put into his agricultural arts. I complimented him, but I'm not sure he even heard me. He was now repeating a script, well-rehearsed, that had been heard, no doubt, by many a visitor! One glance at the driver, standing by dutifully, confirmed my suspicion. "Gentlemen, true beauty is never separate from utility. Only those possessed of a modicum of sagacity will understand this." Apparently this was his closing line, as he wheeled around and strode over to the cart. The driver had jumped up on his perch at the first mention of "the beauty of utility." The performance was over.

As we meandered down the hill to the property, Paul remarked, "Quintilian, I admire any man who can take joy in the work of his hands, and spread that joy to those who are in his hire as well as those who benefit from his labor." "Thank you, Paul. I am so proud of this place." It showed. "And, oh how I wish I never had to leave here. You are right! *This* is where life is lived well. As I have repeated numerous times, the heart of the country is where 'the holy people grow.' But, alas, another principle is at play here. For, as the Greeks maintain, especially Aristotle, humans are social. This place is isolated, and I, for one, am a very social animal." "As am I, friend. As am I." Paul echoed his previous sentiment, in part, to demonstrate that he was

---

2. These lines are appropriated, verbatim, from Quintilian's great work, *Institutes of Oratory.*

listening, "Holy people need others on whom to practice holiness!" "Ha! Well said! And the well-ordered state is not unlike this well-ordered operation; the many disparate parts are ordered around central principles. They operate, more-or-less independently of each other, but together, all function in an organic, harmonious whole." Now he was talking Paul's language. "Fascinating. Yessss. . . . Each 'member,' so to speak, contributes freely, for the well-being of the whole, and the Logos orders all that 'motion'; in a word, concord."

Although the "disputatio" was tiresome to me, I do enjoy recounting how the "muses of this place" inspired Paul to, without effort, think analogically across industry, nature, political thought, social organization, and I never tire of learning how all that relates to the 'Body of Christ.' Imagination is a wonderful thing. Quintilian continued. "Yes, indeed. I see the comparison. Social harmony is a beautiful dream. I wish to note, particularly, the centrality of 'Logos,' of word, in your vision. Ants are organized by some mysterious, outward force. Slaves are not free to organize themselves, but are told what to do, when to do it, and where. It is the free man, the free society, that needs most the power of rhetoric to organize. Where the role of rhetoric is neglected, civil society cannot exist. Rhetoric draws free men to freely embrace those principles that order their lives, that improve their lives, and build bonds of community."

Paul was deeply impressed by this profound insight. The driver urged the horses on; Quintilian continued. "Illiberal societies care nothing for rhetoric. When you persuade the other person, he remains free. However, if one requires only simple obedience, coercion suffices. Free persons ought always relate to one another on the basis of persuasion, which presupposes mutual respect, integrity, and trust. This is the province of rhetoric. So, you see, rhetoric abides at the core of our culture."

"This is a hopeful and lofty view of rhetoric. I must admit, I am in the habit of viewing rhetoric more in terms of its abuses at the hands of Sophists." "As do most." "But your view comports with my own view of social harmony, based on the teachings of Christ, that I embrace." "Really? Then why have so many Christians joined that dreadful revolt?"

"That is a discussion, friend," Paul shook his head in consternation, "that will require a great deal of time, and one or two glasses of your Rioja wine! Ha!" The stable master met us at the gate, took the reins and sent the driver to the kitchen. All thanked him for safe travels. "Welcome home, Master!"

11

The Grand Tour

Calagurritanum (near Calagurris, in La Rioja, where Rio Cidacos joins Rio Iberus)

IF THERE WERE TWO facets of his operation about which Quintilian is passionate, they are his horse breeding and his winery. Oh, and his mining operation! "There is the mine again. See . . . no, there, there!" Paul strained a little harder. "Sorry, my eyesight is not so good." "We mine gold and silver both, right over there and smelt it, on the edge of the property, below the mine, by the river where we have plenty of water. We embellish the villa, make silverware, goblets and plates, even attach to fine steel blades from Toletum, the complete hilt: guard, grip, and pommel." As he said this, Quintilian drew his sword and displayed it for our consideration. "The finest shops in Toletum look to us to embellish their hilts." "I understand why! Beautiful, beautiful, work." "Thank you. Anyway, we cast up the excess into ingots." Paul nodded, but was thinking of his next move. I recognized the look. Quintilian explained something very technical about how they imported a new fuel for smelting and forging that burned hotter than wood. "We buy it by the ship load, from away up north, beyond Gaul."

Quintilian was either oblivious to Paul's lack of attention, or simply trudged forward out of habit. "The horses," he exclaimed, overcome with admiration, "*these horses*, have been carefully bred from the *finest* stock of the Baetis valley, you know, Corduba?" "Yes. I know *of* it," I replied. "There," combing the long, dark gray mane, "in Corduba, well, . . ." he pats the horse's neck, "there are no finer horses in all Hispania! You know, we spoke of the relation of beauty to utility? Consider how the horse that has thin flanks is thought handsomer than one of a different shape, and is *also* more swift. It is not unlike the soldier whose muscles have been developed by exercise. He is both pleasing to the eye, and is, by virtue of the exercise, so much the better prepared for combat. Beauty and utility; utility and beauty, you see? Anyway, I am the only horseman in the Seven Valleys to breed these beautiful animals!" "Well, I know nothing of horses," Paul admitted, "but I know a beautiful animal when I see one! And proud!"

Paul made his move. "Socrates was a soldier, but the weapons of his warfare were of a different sort." Quintilian was clearly jarred by Paul's abrupt change of direction, but played along nonetheless. "Chief among these were 'Eristic.' He supposed that, by teaching eristic to the youth of Athens, they would be 'fit for the battle of ideas.'" "Yes. He lived and died by eristic."

P: What did Afer teach you about eristic?

Q: He taught, first of all, that what Plato called 'eristic,' Aristotle called 'dialectic.'

P: I learned the same in my school. I was thinking more in terms of methodology?

Q: Well, there are two disputants. They agree upon a thesis. They conduct an inquiry regarding this thesis, one person upholding it, the other asking questions.

P: Yes.

Q: According to Afer, the other disputant asks questions in order to get his interlocutor to arrive at a contradiction. When a contradiction is arrived at, there are but two conclusions: Either the thesis is wrong or the person defending it made an error.

P: Yes, Aristotle, in his *Topica*, called this "Elenchus"-that point at which you arrive at the contradiction.

Q: And, when eristic was taught as a game, there was a time limit. You had to make your opponent arrive at a foolish statement in so many minutes.

Quintilian was growing impatient.

P: Indeed!

Q: So, what? Why bother with child's play?

Paul was on the verge of making his reply when I interrupted. "Such a nice garden! You grow many healing herbs, I see." On our way to the stable, we came upon a small herb garden. I was not only disinterested in the methodology of eristic, I was anxious to change the subject. "Yes," said Quintilian. "Luke, do you know what is behind that door?" I shook my head, but I had my hopes. "That is our dispensary. We are doing some intensive studies with a number of remedies and compounds. Would you like to take a look?" "Would I?" I went inside, waving as I closed the door behind me. "Ah, peace at last." It's not that I didn't enjoy their talk . . . yes it was.

Paul and Quintilian made their way to the stable, just beyond the dispensary.

P: But, friend, neither am I interested in games, in 'child's play.' Especially now! I have so little time. I must "be about my Master's business." And recall, how in his *Topics*, Aristotle also pointed out that dialectic was more than just a game for schoolboys? That, beyond intellectual sparring, it is a means of organizing the search for truth?

Q: Indeed, I do. That it is useful, not only for the mutual search for truth, but for individuals, as well.

P: Right! I've always been captivated most by his claim that dialectic is a "process of criticism wherein lies the path to the principles of all inquiries."

Q: Absolutely! We are similarly motivated, friend. This facet of Aristotle's dialectic has wide and serious application, both in questions of public policy making and in private choice; for cultivation of both civic and of private virtue.

P: Take, for instance, this horse over here. Suppose you groomed him for a show, and you braided his mane such that it looked effeminate; with little bows and flowers all woven in.

Q: Ha! I see where you are going with this. Absurd!

P: Absurd, why?

Q: Because it diminishes or is at odds with his pride; his high spirits.

P: And why should that matter?

Q: Because much of the beauty of the animal is derived from the way he carries himself, namely, with pride and dignity.

P: Yes. So it follows, does it not, that beauty and stateliness, or dignity, or "gravitas," are closely related, insofar as show animals are concerned?

Q: Indeed.

P: But, when it comes to ideas, especially ideas concerning matters of faith, that are of utmost importance, ridiculous embellishment and exaggerated adornment could in no way encourage an audience to take seriously ideas so adorned and so embellished?

Q: I can think of no better way, Paul, to cast up one's doctrine . . . (here came a strategic pause) if one were running a school for clowns!

Quintilian could not help but guffaw at his own wit.
    Paul said, also amused,

P: Couldn't have said it better myself.

Q: But surely you recognize a legitimate use of humor and exaggeration, as Aristotle discusses in the Second Book of his *Poetics*?

P: No, I am very wary, in fact, of falling into the trap of an overwrought or effeminate mode of communicating Divine Truth. It seems reckless and irresponsible.

Q: I agree with you, Paul, very much so, but, surely, there is a place for vivid mental imagery? Surely it is appropriate, even when discussing the gravest of matters, to introduce some distorted imagery, for the sake of levity? Not to mention the importance of the artful, deliberate use of the crescendo, parallelism, antithesis, hyperbole, and the like. Without these rhetorical figures, the eristic treatment of ideas, the dialectic, would simply drone on in monotonous regularity. How could ideas expounded with such little imagination possibly prevail?

P: Well, now that you mention it, I do love a well-timed, periodic sentence!

Q: I appreciate hearing this admission from your own lips. Otherwise, I would have been forced to point out to you that the mental image of that particular horse, all coiffed and manicured, was absurd and humorous, and it *served a serious point*! Quite well in fact.

"By the way, did you realize, Paul, that, if I have my man gather the horse droppings from the stable, then spread them over my grain fields, I can significantly increase yields?" "Fascinating." (He took a moment to catch up.) "Is there some sort of transference of the life force from the decaying excrement to the seed, in the soil? What do you think is happening there? How do you know the yields are increased?"

"I suspect the dung introduces heat into the soil that is conducive to the seedling's growth, so that more of them take root than would be the case without the dung. We are still working out the science of it." "We must speak more of this scientific approach to farming."

Q: And so we shall! At any rate, back to your serious point: I was re- minded of the discussion in Plato's *Phaedrus*, between feigned beauty and true beauty; between make up and exercise; between flattery and truth-telling.

P: Good. That is what I was getting at! Sophists flatter the audience for unsavory motives. This affects the auditors the same way face paint produces feigned beauty, by imitating good health.

Q: Yes, reliance on face paint for the appearance of health, without the benefit of exercise, leads, in the end, to ill health, and to vain attempts to "dress up" an old and obviously unhealthy visage. It is grotesque; decidedly not beautiful, just as it is not good to overdress ideas. If bad ideas masquerade as good ones, and citizens "swallow" them, they will eventually develop a diseased soul. Sham truth can never produce a healthy soul.

This last assertion convinced Paul at once. Still, he will not allow him- self to be swept away by the elegance of the argument. He is a discriminating lover of Truth! "But, unlike Plato, rather than passing off 'horse droppings' as truth," Paul winked at his new best friend, "we were talking about adorning *Truth*. And, in the process, we touched on the nature of true Beauty."

Q: Yes, we were.

P: So, friend, I ask you, where is the mean between buffoonery and the dry exposition of Truth? I am convinced, because God's Truth is associated, throughout scripture, with life-giving streams of water, that my compositions should be lively. However, I have never been comfortable utilizing large numbers of figures. Don't such fanciful constructions come off as flowery or contrived; too "bubbly?" I want to avoid sacrificing substance for mere rhetoric!

Q: "Mere rhetoric." What is that, really? Don't the best orators always strive to make beautiful arguments that have passed the muster of dialectical scrutiny, and don't they cast up their rhetoric with eloquence and vivacity, by maintaining propriety, decorum, and perspicuity?

P: Well said. I strive to do no less.

Q: In fact, I would go so far as to say that attempts to persuade one's fellows which are constructed of untruth, because they could potentially warp the soul of one's fellows, does not rightly constitute rhetoric, at all. By virtue of a faulty moral aim, or by employing untruth or extreme exaggeration, the persuasion changes, in kind, and ought properly, rather than "rhetoric," be thought of as "bombast," or "sophistry."

P: Interesting. I suppose this is so. . . .

Q: Of course it is so. I decided, long ago, that rhetoric should be understood, in its fullness, and within its proper sphere, as grounded in truth-telling. It is ethical, "all the way down," as it were. Oh, Afer and I used to get into it. . . .

P: Ha! Intriguing. I have always viewed rhetoric as an amoral tool, like a sword, that can be used for good or for ill. Seems to me that most use it as a tool of self-advancement.

Q: Man is not merely a mind that walks about! He has a soul. To appeal to his feeling, to his heart, is therefore not necessarily an insult! Rhetoric recognizes man in the fullness of his being!

P: I admit, I've always felt that to appeal to his feelings was a disservice to man; that it is best to confine oneself to appeals to reason!

Q: Don't provoke me, Paul! (Quintilian shook his fist in feigned anger. This was, in fact, one of his great frustrations concerning his chosen profession.) Many feel that way. But I maintain that rhetoric speaks to man in his whole being and out of his whole past and with reference to values which only a human being can intuit.[1]

P: I can see great possibilities for this view of rhetoric to enhance my work, building up the faithful. These possibilities are staggering, in fact!

Q: Indeed! *Any* community is strengthened as its common values are replenished, rehearsed, and reclaimed! This is the "cultural role of rhetoric." Crafting speeches is the superficial, technical use of rhetoric. The premises upon which a speech is based, the materials which must be mined from the very depths of the place about which one aims to speak, these constitute the heart of the place. And they are not evoked in some silly and direct fashion. They are "presuppositious"; left unspoken. They are "enthymematic." They have to do with what we assume is Good when we are not discussing what is Good, but are focused rather, on a particular good. When we do this, we share our values. The auditor must embrace our view of the Good in order to make sense of our pronouncements about the particular good. If we share these views, we are in community; if we do not, we are without. We are *barboroi*.

P: Fascinating. So, does this have anything to do with the orator being "vir bonus"; the "good man" about which you spoke on the road, yesterday? Did you not say, if he is not a good man, he subverts communal bonds?

Q: Precisely. For the well-being of society, he must be a good man and must feel the "pull" of the fist principles that form the wellsprings of the society in which he leads. If he does not feel them, if he does not participate in that "*common unity*" he is an outsider.

Paul's eyes are fully opened.

P: This is an elevated conception of rhetoric, indeed.

Q: It is, I believe, what Plato had in mind when he wrote his *Phaedrus*.

---

1. Here I have Quintilian speak the words of Richard M. Weaver, from the conclusion of, "The Cultural Role of Rhetoric." Weaverian thought shapes a good deal of the dialogue in this work.

P: Hmmm.

Q: Because, friend, it takes a "vir bonus," a good man, to engage in true
rhetoric.

P: I perceive our dialectic just took a turn back toward the consideration
of Truth, Beauty, and Goodness! We are come full circle!

Q: Wha—?

P: Remember, back in Tarraco? We were discussing that line my friend
attributed to you.

Q: Oh, of course. Yes!

P: And what of you, friend?

Q: What of me?

He had no idea what Paul was getting at.

P: To what extent is your interest in the arts of rhetoric fueled by such
grand, beautiful and good service to your fellows?

Quintilian had no ready answer.

P: . . . or, to what extent is your interest in rhetoric fueled by your desire
for fame?

Q: Please, let's make our way to the veranda to entertain that question
over a glass of wine!

He said "glass" but mimed the action of one drinking from an oversized
wineskin!

P: Lead the way!

Q: Ha! Yes!

Just at the door of the barn, an olive skinned, dark haired, young
Spaniard—or was he African?—some sort of implement in hand, appeared
and bowed to Quintilian, "Excuse me, Sir. Africanus dropped by to see if
you have any instructions for him before you leave?" "Thank you, Stable
Master, but I am presently unavailable," he pointed to us, indicating that
he had company. "Please have him visit with Darío. He understands better
than I what is required. But, please impress on them both that it is critical
that the four varieties of grapes be handled separately, logged carefully as
each cask is racked, and the results meticulously catalogued before the end

of *each* workday without fail. Otherwise, all my years of hard work could be in vain, simply because I am not here to keep an eye on things," he spelled it out to all present, no doubt in hopes that many witnesses would produce increased vigilance. Turning to Paul, he said, "The only operation for which I have as much care is the mining and smelting, but for different reasons. The winery is a *labor of love*, and one of the only areas in my life where I aim at perfection. It is not an indulgence, it is the operation from which I derive greatest joy." Then, turning back to the Stable Master, with a stern, practiced eye, he warned, "so, if it is botched while I am away, to the degree it is botched, to that same degree I shall demand an accounting! Impress that upon Africanus for me, won't you?" The Stable Master, as he retreats, bows, and replies with practiced deference, "Yes, sir. It shall be done precisely as you wish. I shall see to it myself."

"Okay. To the veranda for that glass of wine. It is just around the corner there, past the portico to the courtyard." Paul tried to keep up and exclaimed, "You are a busy young man!" Quintilian replied, "I would like nothing more than to be transported out of here! Interruptions, interruptions, and more interruptions!"

Something in the exchange between the stable master and Quintilian prompted Paul to continue the story of his conversion, which he had started to share on the road, earlier. "I never got to elaborate on my conversion story. We were sidetracked."

"Oh, by all means." Quintilian was agreeable.

"On the road to Damascus it was. I was on my way to lock up some Christians, in fact!"

"You don't say!?" Quintilian relished the irony.

"I was knocked off my donkey . . ."

"You rode a donkey? Ha."

"Yes. The chief priests wanted to keep me humble."

Many years had passed; Paul now saw the humor in it. He stopped to smile, then cleared his throat and continued. "I was taken to a believer's house in Damascus, according to the voice . . . "

"*Voice?*"! Quintilian required clarification. This was fantastic. "I was blinded and a voice addressed me, personally, nobody else understood it—" Projecting feigned skepticism (which, by the way, was lost on Paul,) Quintilian asked, "*Nobody* else heard this voice? Ha!" "No, I said they did not *understand* it. They heard it alright. May I continue?" "Sorry."

"Anyway, it commanded me to go to the house of Ananias, a Believer, and he would pray for me. That voice identified himself to me as 'Jesus, whom you persecute.'"

"Oh, my! That sounds terrifying." (There was nothing feigned about this response. Quintilian had grown genuinely interested.)

"No, it was not a pleasant experience. So, I did as I was instructed, then, after yielding to his calling, I went to the wilderness for a season, and the same voice, the voice of God's Only Son, unfolded to me the scriptures concerning himself."

"What scriptures?"

"Torah, Prophets, and Psalms. Everything concerning his conception by the Holy Spirit, His virgin birth, His being a spotless lamb, without sin, who came to take away the sin of the world, how His kingdom was not of this world, how He wants us to love and serve one another, and love God with our whole mind, heart, and strength. Everything. And so, my dear Quintilian, the Jews hate me on account of my conversion, the Jewish Christians hate me on account of the persecution, and the ones who forgave me for *that* think I am pompous to claim that I was taught directly by Christ, even though it is true! I think there are very few Jews who care for me . . . no. No, there are *none*!"

Qunitilian had to do a double take. Paul was smirking directly at him, a twinkle in his eye! "Ha! *That* is hilarious!"

Quintilian had halted by the portico to give Paul a look at the vineyard. He spoke loudly, because the fountain in the courtyard behind them gurgled noisily. The vineyard spread out below the veranda, and disappeared away over a hill, into the elms and cypress that grew thick on the Iberus bottom lands. Quintilian pointed to the orange rocky crags rising out of the trees across the river, beyond the vineyard and beyond the fields. Following the river with his outstretched hand, from south to north, our host said, "See how the river forms an omega-shape, there and, looping around to there, beyond the apple orchard? Those are the borders of Calagurritanum, on *this* side of the river! Across the river, where the mine is situated, we own another 60 hectares. My family owns all the land south of Rio Cidacos, from that huge boulder we passed, remember? with the cedar growing on top of it, south, in a straight line, as far as one can walk in half a day, then, back to the river!"

Paul gazed off toward the horizon, tilted his head slightly, as he did when collecting his thoughts. As he scratched his nose with his pointer finger, he froze. Away off toward the crags, he saw a hawk circling, then gliding along the foothills. Mesmerized, he traced its movement. "Beautiful," he thought. Perhaps it was the gurgling of the fountain, or the warm afternoon breeze on his face, or the motion of the hawk, or all these but, slowly, closing his eyes, head tilted back and to the side, as intellect yields to memory and imagination, he is transported through time, to his youth, back home in Tarsus, when he was captivated, with something akin to intellectual curiosity, by a scene much like this one. It was the same time of day. He had been out for a walk with his father, learning flora and fauna. Father took keen interest in his son's knowledge of the natural world, "Our Heavenly Father's beautiful creation," he always called it. "It brings the Most High great glory, my son, when we learn the names of things passed down since the Garden."

Father had been drilling me on the names of trees, Paul concentrated, sharpening, filling out, and adding color to the mental image forming in his mind's eye. Yes . . . we were at the goat farm, checking the progress of the new herdsman. Up the river Cydnus. Always loved those trips with father. We were on our way back to town. He sat me up on a large, flat rock, up that little ravine just to the north of the university. We were taking a break to eat something, on the rock. Half in and half out of the river, it was. I had just taken a handful of almonds into my mouth and, when I began to chew them, I spied the hawk, off to the west . . . gliding away to the south, along the foothills, late afternoon, it was. A long time I forgot to chew, only watched. The sky was a particularly spectacular azure that day. Bright and clear, no cloud in the sky. Nothing but that hawk. Now gliding, now circling; ever watching. Hungry. Searching, then circling back.

Apollos came to mind. Paul had been enjoying the way the gulls glided along behind the ship, then flew up to see if they could coax a scrap of something, on the voyage from Ostia, when Apollos interrupted. The gulls were nowhere near as graceful as the hawks. What was it Apollos had said? "Surely you should put your name to it! You were taught by Christ Jesus himself. You are an apostle of distinction. No other apostle can claim this!"

"Are you with me, Paul?" The hawk was gone. Fully present once again, Paul explained, "Oh, I just saw a hawk off there on the horizon. It took me back to my youth, in Tarsus, with my father, along the River Cydnus. This area quite resembles it; so beautiful!" "A hawk, you say? On the horizon, over there, near the foothills? Gliding, was it? Heading due West?" This was odd. "Uh . . . yes. Yes, it was." "I dreamt this two nights ago. In my dream,

I was transported to *my* youth by the sight of *that* hawk, standing on this very spot." He pointed to the spot where we stood, for emphasis. Smiling, Paul asked, "Oh, very interesting. What do you think it means?" "That Fortune is smiling on us, I guess? I just find it fascinating, though, how one can be transported, in the mind's eye, in the blink of an eye, to places in the memory. Sometimes these sensations are so vivid; so real." . . . From beyond the river, in the direction of the mine, came the most haunting, beautiful sound. Nine times it sounded, coming in distinct, precise, lengthy intervals. It drew me out of the dispensary to where they stood. "What was that?" I inquired. "A 'bell,' Quintilian explained, "Made of iron, shaped more-or-less like a cone, as tall as a man. I have the minekeeper strike it with a small log lashed to a fulcrum, each hour so the entire valley knows the time of day. It is precisely the ninth hour." Anticipating my next question, "he has a sundial."

"Yesssss," Paul trailed his "s" to signal both deep agreement with Quintilian's previous remark, and wonderment at the sound that had just sidetracked us. "Such is the excellence of rhetoric, is it not? To craft an idea so lively, so vivid, that the auditors can 'see and feel' details of a past experience, or maybe, through the aid of fancy, picture a place they have never even been!" "Indeed! And these experiences always spur other thoughts; other memories, or analogous experiences. I suppose that is the aim for which you labor most, in your line of work: Helping your converts imagine what heaven is like?" "True," Paul agreed. "Any number of senses can trigger fond or striking memories, the way the smell of baking bread reminds most of grandmother's kitchen; 'takes one back' to a pleasant season of life."

Q: Yes. This is one facet of happiness in life. Those fond memories, the most lively ones, impress upon the soul how life can be beautiful when one is faced daily with ugliness and evil fortune. I wonder if these considerations are what Plato had in mind when, in his *Phaedrus* he urged that rhetoric should be grounded in the study of the soul?

P: This is most certainly true. Rhetoric, along the lines envisaged by Plato (and elaborated in Aristotle,) does humanity a great service insofar as, on the one hand, it brings to mind pleasant times (coupled with the hope that they can be pleasant again,) and, on the other hand, of times as yet unseen, but believed in, nonetheless.

Q: Faith.

P: Yes. Faith. Faith is, as the song goes,

the substance of things hoped for; the evidence of things not seen.

Q: That's nice. You should work that into your little manuscript, there.

Quintilian returned to the script one suspected he used for every tour he provided every guest. "You know, seeing that mine across the river there, reminds me that, as one composes an argument, each nugget of truth points to a vein, and following that vein, which is very hot, difficult work, is the only way to extract the real treasure, hidden in the deep. But even after all that intense labor, the miner must 'remove the dross' to increase the value of the treasure. This is much like dialectic and rhetoric. Dialectic is the implement by which the work is done. Rhetoric provides the drive to extract the treasure, because the vision of the beauty of what can be done with the gold, or the silver, motivates the miner to follow the vein and remove the dross. And then there is the problem of 'fool's gold'!" Paul yawned. "So, what you are saying is that, to continue with our discussion of Truth, Beauty, and Goodness, dialectic and rhetoric work together, much as Aristotle noted in the opening line of his *Rhetorica*?" "Indeed." "That dialectic and rhetoric are 'antistrophes,' or 'counterparts,' of one another?" "Yes, Señor Paul. And truth-telling is a prime concern of the "good man speaking well," because he wishes to make his auditors better people." Quintilian took a few steps up the stairs to the veranda.

"Well, if you don't mind, Sir, I shall retire to my room for a little nap and see you after the heat of the day passes." Quintilian asked if he would like to go for a ride around the villa before supper. Paul turned down his offer, saying he also needed to write down some ideas before he forgot them. "You have given me much to contemplate, friend." Quintilian replied, "See you at dinner then, good sir. We will dine at sunset."

⤿

Paul emerged from his room well before sunset; before the table had been set. Quintilian wondered, "I thought you were going to rest, friend?" "Luke is. I couldn't," said Paul. "Too excited. We've discussed so much and I can't get your last point out of my mind!" Quintilian listened attentively, but, at the same time, made eye contact with his attendant, discreetly bringing his fingertips to his lips then indicating with a nod of the head that, although dinner wasn't for another hour, he wished to provide for his guest an afternoon snack.

One plank at a time, Meats, breads, cheese, fruits and nuts were set before them, with a silver goblet of sweet red wine. Paul gave up trying to speak after the second plank. There was a hard, pungent white cheese and a brown goat cheese with some sort of honey-nut concoction blended in. A sweet pan bread, and a sour one, thinly sliced and lightly toasted were offered, along with oil and vinegar for dipping and smoked ham and lamb slices to complement the cheese. Apple slices, grapes, and candied almonds. Three varieties of olives and dried tomatoes completed the fare. Paul had not had time to eat much this day. He hadn't realized how hungry he was, until now!

Paul, quite forgetting his manners, expressed gratitude while simultaneously filling his mouth, drinking, *and* giving thanks to God! "Won't you offer a prayer of thanksgiving for us both?" Quintilian's invitation took Paul by surprise. Blushing, he gulped, cleared his throat, wiped his mouth, and began again, "Forgive me, Sir. I fear I've let my appetite get the best of me." He said a common prayer, then said, "I realized, as the food arrived, I barely ate today! Barely ate yesterday, come to think of it! Thank you. This is exquisite! Especially the olives. Yes, and the cheeses! Marvelous." Quintilian replied, simply, "The pleasure is all mine, Paul. While we enjoy our little snack, I have a question about praying. When Christians pray, asking God to 'forgive us our sins as we forgive others,' what does this mean? Isn't God the only one who can forgive sins?"

Up to that point, Paul was paying more attention to the food than to gratifying his guest's curiosity. But the profundity of the question his host asked stopped Paul in the middle of chewing his food! This was *not* idle curiosity. "Well, Quintilian, you are correct. God only can forgive sins that relate to our juridical standing before the Lawgiver. In this prayer, which, by the way, was taught by Jesus, in response to his disciples' request that he teach them to pray, in this prayer, we understand that we beg our Father in heaven to not look at our sins, or deny our prayer because of them. We learn that we are neither worthy of the things for which we pray, nor have we deserved them, but we ask that He would give them all to us by grace, for we daily sin much and surely deserve nothing but punishment. Which is why we, in turn, sincerely forgive and gladly do good to those who sin against us, expecting nothing in return."

All during Paul's explanation, Quintilian slowly chewed small handfuls of food, washing each down with a sip of wine, all the while staring, contemplatively, off into the twilight forming to the East. He responded, only once, "Thank you. Well spoken." He meant to "ruminate" on Paul's explanation, as he was fond of saying. When Paul had finished he said, "Please, Paul, tell me more about your manuscript?"

"Looking back, it seems I have painted each of my letters, for the most part, from the same palette, so to speak. They are fine. They have texture, they have substance, they have depth. But they are all so similar. I am inclined, before I die in Rome, to leave a magnum opus. My friends in Rome are having such a difficult time of it. I want to encourage, uh, give them something extraordinary so they feel extraordinarily encouraged." "Why don't you give me a concrete example. Perhaps I can help."

"Certainly. Christians are in a precarious position throughout Rome."

"So, I've noticed."

"Right. Being called to spread teachings of Jesus of Nazareth among the Gentiles, as I, I tend to emphasize how they have been 'grafted into the body,' as it were. Jews are, well, I don't have to tell you how they look down on the *barbaroi.*"

"I am aware of their reputation in this regard, yes."

"So I usually tend to emphasize that the wall of division between them has been torn down in the eyes of God, then, in virtually all my other letters, I include a section in which I discuss that inter-relation in terms of a 'body' metaphor. That we are the body of Jesus, in the earth. That we have one faith; one confession; one spirit. That we represent him, corporately, in our relations one to another, and that, in order to do so with utmost efficacy, we ought to relate to one another in love, serving one another. The difference now, of course, being that I wish to direct this work to my kinsmen, so none of this really applies."

"So," Quintilian asks the obvious question, "what would be so difficult about taking a different tack in this letter? I don't see where you need my help?" "Yes, well, I am not satisfied to simply take a different tack, in terms of content. Regarding substance I need no help. It's the *style* I wish to make a distinguishing trait of this letter, and, frankly, style is not my strength!" But *you* are truly gifted in this regard! The pathos you evoke is magnificent! Why, in that Provincial Court the other day, I was angry at the witness myself! er, that Sabinus! Yes, I wanted to lock *him* up, and I had only walked in as you were concluding! And therein lies the problem. When I consider my own reaction, I worry that persons can become intoxicated on the beauty of the words, which diminishes the actual potency of the words; that the artistry resembles more harlotry than beauty, more window dressing than true elegance. I, myself, fear that I am, at times, prone to this impropriety, and I certainly have colleagues, one in particular, who strikes me as rather smitten with his own clever use of words." Paul's conduct toward Apollos now embarrassed him. He would have to have a word with him when they gathered in Caesaraugusta.

"Yes, I suppose every art is open to abuse, but surely you agree, Paul, that, once . . . " Paul continued, Quintilian had mistaken his momentary pause for the conclusion of a thought but it was, in fact, simply the beginning of a segue, " . . . *which* begs an important question for me regarding the difference between persuasion and preaching. In my parlance, I can see where persuasion is indispensable in apologia, when spreading the good news among those who've not yet heard. But my letters I write for the benefit of those *already* in The Way; who've already started down that path."

"Certainly," replied Quintilian, "docere versus movere."

"Yes. I've heard this teaching. So," said Paul, pausing for a long draft from his goblet, "when one's aim is instruction, it seems proper, as is commonly taught, that one refrain from rhetorical flourishes and speak in plain style."

"Generally, I would agree, friend. But you are not writing to a general audience, and part of your aim is rhetorical, is it not?"

Q: So, what obstacle, in the nature of the Hebrew people, must you address in order to move them toward your position?

Quintilian, barely audible, chuckled to himself. The implication of his own question dawning on him in the asking.

P: We are "a stiff-necked people."

We saluted our agreement with raised goblets.

P: Ha! Yes. Don't I know they, er *we*, are a stiff-necked people. So, I suppose a few images will go a long way in overcoming that resistance to the truth that characterized through the ages our response to God's messengers!

Q: I believe so, yes. You wish to make this letter distinct from the others. Gripping the readers' reason is one thing. Captivating their imagination, which is the only way to penetrate the hard shell, that is another! "Form and function!" So, again, what is needed?

Paul scratched his chin then took another drink of wine, popped a date in his mouth and chewed it, pensively. Ew. They did *not* go well together. "Well, I suppose the Jews are a warrior nation, so I could utilize battle metaphors." "Yes, but you already used that metaphor in your letter to the Roman Christians, did you not?"

"Drat! *And* in the 'full armor' allegory at the conclusion of the letter to the church at Ephesus. It seems I am in the habit of drawing my illustrations from either battle or from foot races." "Is there no *rest* involved in service to your God?" Paul only nodded, alternated his gaze from the vineyard to the sky above, scratching his temple. Pursuing an idea like the one to which he had locked on, rendered speech superfluous. So Quintilian continued, which launched Paul onto a train of thought that occupied him the next several hours. "Doesn't that 'New Covenant' of which you spoke offer any rest? On our way here, you kept talking about the need to rest from our labors. Jews strive to please God more than any other people on earth, no?"

Paul replies, simply, "Absolutely." He is still nodding, but doesn't realize it.

Q: Well, then, is there any sort of exhortation you could employ that would appeal more deeply to your kinsmen than "rest," what with all the agitation and zealotry consuming them at present?

P: Hmmmm . . . qood question. "Rest, yes, I suppose."

Q: Rest. Rest from revolting against Roman rule so strenuously?

P: No, against a different "Empire."

Paul was being clever. His imagination was now flooded with possibilities.

P: And I could replace all the maritime nonsense with a line about the Sabbath Rest of God. Jews have a keen interest in realizing the promised Sabbath Rest.

"Ah, I see your intention. Spot on."

"I think I could have an entire opening movement in which I discuss 'entering His Rest,' and how the hardness of one's heart prevents one from entering it."

"Yes, absolutely. And you could say something like, 'Let us strive to enter that rest. . . .' Employ an antithesis, even. That would be striking, no?"

"I suppose. *'Strive to enter that rest.'* . . . I will have to toy with that a bit. That may be a little trite." Paul was not really sold on this idea.

"Well, at any rate, I think this is a very good idea."

"Indeed it is. Give me a moment, here, to jot down a few thoughts."

"Certainly." Quintilian poured another goblet of wine. He was pleased to have been some help.

"Alright, then. There is a Sabbath rest that may appeal to the children of Israel?"

Paul replies simply, "Absolutely . . . " trailing off in deep thought.

"I should think it would be gripping to most readers to read an antithesis to the effect that one needs to 'strive to enter that rest.' I know I, for one, take great comfort resting in the blessings of the gods." "Yes, but, resting in the good works of one's own hands—" "Paul, friend, we've been through this already. 'Faith, duty, spirit.' These are the pillars of my religion. Is there not a universal aspect, common to all religions, of 'striving to enter god's rest'? Don't all religions teach that we find rest for our weary soul, once we have striven to overcome our sins with good works, thus finding favor with god?"

"You see, my friend, this is the sticking point. As I'm sure you noticed in what you have read, all the good works in the world are insufficient to purchase divine approval. Jesus paid the price, on the cross of Calvary, and he gives, freely, salvation to all who believe in Him, confess and repent of their sins, and are baptized. This is what he commands." "See now, that last part, that is a good work. You Christians are so deluded!" "No, I am afraid not. It is His work, as well. We enter His rest by accepting His way."

Quintilian was getting flushed again . . . and defensive. "I have all the rest I need. I give of my wealth, I give of the first fruits of my crops, I help the poor, I give of my talents to help those in need, I visit the unfortunates in prison who seek justice! I can think of nothing for which I need to confess before my gods, or any other god, for that matter! I am at rest *because I do good works!* Any god who would make further demands is cruel!"

Paul looked at Quintilian with deep compassion and said, simply, "Friend, to confess your sin is to cease self-justification. Guilt before God Almighty is not a feeling, it is a matter of Law. Therefore, as you, of all men should know, the response to confession is absolution, from the Law-Giver, and *that absolution* is the basis of rest and 'peace that passes understanding.'" "Well, you're right about one thing. I do not understand it. I am a righteous man. Ask anyone." Paul uttered the only three words he needed to utter, then let it go, " . . . *no not one.*"

Striding up to the table, I side-stepped from plank to plank, picking through the leftovers. The tension was palpable. Neither man said a thing, so I broke the ice, "Did you realize Celsus spent 30 years compiling the knowledge in that Encyclopedia of his!? Extraordinary. I'm learning so much about modern medicine." "So glad to hear it," replied Quintilian. "Well," my plate was piled high, my goblet refilled, "back to it!"

Perhaps it was the wine. Perhaps it was the hour. They both dropped it cold. Quintilian renewed the discussion. "What about the forebears?" "What about them?" "There is another, positive, defining characteristic of the Hebrews: That they are mindful of those who walked before them; showed the way. Can that be exploited to good effect?" "I love it! I could envision a section devoted to recapitulating the great achievements of Abraham, Isaac, and Jacob. Oh, and Noah, and Moses, and . . . " Paul was now in the throes of a burst of creativity like he had never experienced before. Quintilian had another thought, but Paul had already stood, grabbed a last chunk of cheese to eat later, a handful of almonds, popped these in his mouth, turned on his heal, muttered a word of thanks as he gathered his writing things, and headed for his room.

"Hey, Paul, don't forget what I said about parallelism! If you are going to devote a section to listing the 'Great ones of the faith,' weaving together the entire list with some common refrain, or polysyndeton, would be perfect!" Paul, walks away, mumbling to himself, "I know! 'Let us.' I can repeat 'Let us' exactly 12 times!" This puzzled Quintilian.

"Exactly 12 times? Why so precise a num . . . ?" "Completeness. Um . . . it is numerological," he says, as he wanders off. . . .

Darío wasted no time. He had been waiting patiently, and wished desperately to get home to his family, so he bowed and asked Master Fabius for a minute of his time. He was waving the list of items about which he had questions. "Yes, yes of course. Sorry to keep you waiting so long." Finally, Darío could confirm the disposition of those items which Quintilian intended to pack, and those he intended to leave behind.

12

Rhetoric: The Intellectual Love of God

NEXT MORNING, THEY ARRIVED at the veranda, more or less, at the same time; Paul first, then Quintilian. The bejeweled sunrise greeted him; rubies masking and fusing with a topaz morning sun, mounting an aquamarine sky. "Splendor, majesty, glory . . . " Paul's impulse to praise and thank God was ignited by this breathtaking beauty. As he said his morning prayers, still riveted, Quintilian walked up behind him and asked if he had slept well. Slightly startled, Paul reciprocated, turning, "Ha, ha. Once my mind settled down, yes. I wrote well into the morning hours! and you?" "I am so pleased to know our discussion helped move along your project," Quintilian said. "I slept like a baby. It's the mountain air." "The bit about Melchizedek," Paul exclaimed, "will be excellent. I am supremely satisfied with it. If I . . . " he trailed off as a bit of stray cloud cleared the sunrise, revealing a dazzling display of golden rays that filled the sky. Loud and sustained calls of jackdaws and jays, doves and starlings, and a flock of emerald orange parakeets, blended into a cacophonous chorus of screeches, chirps, and coo-coos. He had to yield. There was no use trying to talk over them, and he wasn't inclined to say anything, anyway. He was listening; savoring.

This was my chance. Under cover of those noisy birds, I snuck up to the table, well behind them, helped myself to a little taste of everything, and stole away undetected, back to the library. I had a date with Celsus!

After a few moments, the birds moved on and Quintilian asked, "So, you were visited by the Muses eh?" "Something like that, yes. As I said, I am very fond of the bit about Melchizedek." "Good, good. Well," Quintilian offered a proper greeting, "good morning! My man has brought some lovely boiled wheat cereal, chopped dates, almonds, figs, and apples, as well as tea, honey, crackers, and goat cheese. Paul, if you please? Let's eat while you report to me your progress?" He seemed earnest; eager to help. Paul seemed eager to share. "One line of which I am particularly proud, which was shaped by our conversations up the Iberus, is: 'He who warps the soul of his audience has no love of neighbor in him.' Another is, 'He who despises his neighbor cannot say, I love God.'" "Well said. I think you will be much happier with these than with your allusion to Sarah and Hagar! Did you come up with a fresh anaphora or two? "Indeed, I did!" Paul was much pleased! "Both as a means of building a shared identity with my kinsmen and as, what you suggested, as a means of unifying the whole, of 'weaving a seamless fabric,' as you put it, I have chosen the refrain, 'Let us.' I like that because, I will make a series of exhortations, but, instead of saying 'you do this' or, 'do that,' I will utilize the kindlier phrase, 'Let us.' It is more importunate than insistent. Each movement will, in fact, begin with the 'Let us' refrain!" "And did you invent any new lines last night?"

Paul was eager to share his night's work. "First, I will establish the problematic, the hardness of the heart, followed by an exhortation to 'Let us encourage one another daily, so we can enter into His Sabbath rest,' then I will stress how they have need of solid meat, but that they are not yet mature enough to handle it, 'Let us move on from milk to solid meat' (a metaphor for the deep things of God,) then, as an example of those deeper things, "Let us" fix our eyes on Jesus who is Both Priest and Sacrifice of the New Covenant, then I discuss briefly the superiority of New Covenant (once for all) and, finally, I plan to return to "this is the basis upon which we can now enter His "Sabbath rest!" And I intend to signal the return to that overarching theme with a *triune* instance of the "Let us" refrain! "I *like* it! Excellent!"

Quintilian had a favorite exercise they used to do at Afer's school that he expected would also benefit Paul. "Is there any chance you could chant it for me, so I can 'take it all in at a glance'? I want to gauge the musicality within the language." "Oh, my goodness. That will be difficult. . . . but I enjoy a good challenge. Interesting, okay. Let's see . . . *Let us* give it a try . . . " (Paul amused himself . . . Despite the fact he already had his eyes closed in concentration, Quintilian caught Paul's little joke, and smiled.) Paul expressed his major themes, accentuating the rhythmic aspects of each phrase. It was helpful, too, because by so doing, he had to, on the spot, think through each point, how they were related, and how they could best be arranged:

So **Let Us** draw near with a true heart,
in full assurance of faith,
with our hearts sprinkled clean from an evil conscience,
and our bodies washed with pure water.

Let us hold fast the confession of our hope without wavering,
for he who promised is faithful.
And—

Let us consider how to stir up one another to love and good works,
not neglecting to meet together, as is the habit of some, but rather
encourage one another,
and all the more as you see the Day draw near.

Paul was self-conscious of his lack of talent for such exercises. "No, no! Well done! Bravo!" Quintilian applauded his effort. You realize, it would take nothing at all to cast up that last phrase as a chiasm?" "Oh, you are right! Wonderful! One of the reasons I got so excited last evening, and wrote all night," Paul paid Quintilian a high compliment, "was because I can picture, in my mind's eye, how very fluid will be the composition based on your recommendations." Quintilian smiled a satisfied smile. "It occurred to me, as well, that the amplification I hope to feature, at the apogee, will be greatly improved by incorporating that series of rhetorical questions you suggested, coupled with an array of anaphoræ and epistrophes." "There is *no doubt* you will have, in hand, your *magnum opus*, when you return to Rome. If you can articulate the nuances of your composition so precisely. . . ." Paul was ecstatic. "You think so? I hope to, by the grace of God, and with your help!"

Bolstered by Paul's appreciation, Quintilian thought of another first rate suggestion. "What if you were to *withhold* your 'Let us' refrain for dramatic effect?" Paul looked at him, a little puzzled. "No, I think not. I am attempting to build a crescendo with the triune, embellished, underscoring of the refrain." "Certainly. I understand. You should do that. Do your didactic best, but then *withhold* the poetic element, for a season, *then*, just at the right moment, repeat it in a *florid* fashion! I do this all the time. It multiplies the effect of the crescendo!" Paul was dumbfounded. He'd never really considered being so deliberate about timing his rhetorical devices for dramatic effect.

Quintilian continued, "I find that, if one attempts to teach fine points of the law to a lay jury, it comes across as condescension. So I set up a cadence by means of epistrophe, repeat a choice phrase at the end of successive points. This gives it a poetic rather than a didactic, feel. Then, I utilize amplification to teach the lesson, while they're in a listening mood, and, for unity's sake, I return to the refrain, repeating it more than once, in quick succession." Quintilian, no doubt due to the glass he had just drained, pounded out the cadence on the table, for effect. Boom! Boom! Boom! "So, you're saying I should develop my doctrine of the priesthood, in plain style, for a season, . . . " "Or some other theme, yes. It doesn't have to be about Melchizedek." " . . . then repeat 'Let us' thrice for emphasis. Yesss . . . "

The layout of the entire treatise had just flashed before him, whole cloth, which he always took to be inspiration from the Holy Spirit. Both the warp, with its foundational color scheme, and the weft, with its detail, down to the headers with each beautiful gold tassel, formed a completed tapestry of God's Truth, in his mind's eye, in half an instant. He paraphrased to confirm understanding, "The rhythm will be established with the "Let us" refrain, early on, then after the didactic 'interlude,' I will return to the "Let us," boom, boom, boom, to herald the return of "Let us encourage one another so our hearts do not become hard" . . . as in the wilderness!! Quintilian! All I can think about now is the beauty of an entire letter, woven seamlessly, start to finish! I think I did that in the argument of the letter to the Romans, but this will be new and different! That one was more syllogistic; this will rely for its force, subtly, on stylistic elegance. That makes so much sense, though, does it not? The Greeks are impressed with logic and, to a lesser extent, with rhetoric. The Jews are moved by ritual and figuration; by allegory and symbolism."

Tossing a date into his mouth, savoring, then washing it down with a draught of sweet, aromatic Mauratanian cardamom tea, Paul exhaled, both from contentment and from mental exhaustion, and, dropping his head, took his seat, across from his host, slowly raising searching eyes to engage Quintilian. This process was hard on an old man! But he could scarcely believe how well it was working; how mightily God was using this time with Quintilian to shape his work.

"Alright," Quintilian, who is ready to get back to work on the manuscript revisions, pushes aside his breakfast plate and settles into his seat. "How did you graft in the Melchizedek branch?" The servant needs no prompting, and clears away the dishes and leftovers. Paul grabs a last gulp of tea, clears his throat and gazes at the morning clouds to gather his thoughts.

"As I said," recounted Paul, "I began with a greeting to the Children of Abraham, talked about the Promises of God, and the need to rest in them, then placed the movement regarding 'A High Priest Forever After the Order of Melchizedek, immediately after that. But it seems somewhat abrupt.'" "A High Priest Forever After the Order of Melchizedek," Quintilian enunciated. "By Jove, that is a beautiful turn of phrase. Is it original?"

"No, it's from the Psalms." "Ah. Pity. We'll address the abruptness in a moment. *Let us* proceed. Heh, heh." "I decided last evening, also, that I needed more scriptural appeals at the outset." "Then this edifice will surely have a solid foundation," said Quintilian, waxing fanciful, swirling his by now cold tea in its goblet, trying to read the leaves. " . . . all bound together with myriad references from the Hebrews' holy book." "Brilliant! And the verse from Psalms that alludes to Melchizedek will be the pivot point. But to what end . . . " Paul tapped his lips with his finger, gripping his chin in thought, gazing once again, heavenward. "Back before the birds interrupted, I started to say, 'If I figure out what end the Melchizedek motif serves.'" Quintilian took the lead.

"Where is that verse placed, at present? Expositio, if you please?"

"Hmmm . . . I discuss with them the need to enter God's Sabbath rest, then propose to talk about the deeper understanding of God's Truth, but chide them for not yet being ready for deeper Truth. I . . . "

Paul, unsure of the accuracy of his recollections, lost his train of thought. "Interesting," Quintilian reassures him. "I believe this is where you removed the bit about Sarah and Hagar?" Paul finished Quintilian's sentence, nodding and gesturing, " . . . and replaced it with the discussion of Melchizedek. You know, come to think of it, I did have a brief allusion, earlier, to the priesthood; that, in the context of not becoming hard-hearted, that believers 'draw near to the Throne of Grace.' Perhaps that will give me a toehold?" "Makes good sense," agreed Quintilian, nodding.

After Paul reviewed the entire middle section of his letter, the great orator nodded with approval and made a final suggestion, "that passage from Psalms that alludes directly to Melchizedek, I would recommend you cite it more than once; for unity's sake. Set up a recurring parallelism." "Very good. Yes, I'd already decided to quote it as a sort of partition. Where else would it fit perfectly? Where is the *kairotic*[1] moment?" "Is there any other scripture that bears repeating? Perhaps you could couple the excerpt from Psalms with another?" Quintilian looked self-satisfied. He knew he was onto something by virtue of Paul's immediate, enthusiastic response!

---

1. Kairos is the Greek term for "timing." Kairos is important because "timing is everything," in teaching as well as in joke telling.

"Of course!! The Annunciation from much earlier, in the second Psalm! It is freshly applied to the Christ, it will speak volumes in this context, and it certainly bears repeating! 'You are my beloved son, Today I have begotten you.' and another, like unto it: 'You are a Priest forever, after the order of Melchizedek.' I quoted the previous passage at the very outset, and it will couple nicely with the former, about Melchizedek, very nicely."

And these will appear together as a segue between the exhortation to "press deeper" and the "deeper truth" regarding the Priesthood after the Order of Melchizedek?

"Yes. Yes they will."

"It sounds to me as though we found what you were looking for!"

"Yes, with the help of God!"

"Of course."

A neighbor from down the road ambled up the lane. Paul excused himself to go wash up, and to fetch Luke for lunch. The servants began setting the table. Without being told, they set a place for Marcellus Vitorius, the neighbor, who had a habit of dropping by at meal time. This neighbor, as it turned out, had ordered several dozen premium grapevines from Burdigala, up in Gaul, and was leaving tomorrow to fetch them, over on the coast somewhere, about a single day's ride. One thing led to another, and he offered us a ride, but Paul declined, saying we were bound to Brigantium.

I confessed to Paul I had started to doubt the wisdom of going all the way to Brigantium. Yes, it was the furtherest point on the map; it was the "Far Shore" of the earth. But, I took him by the arm and led him to the large map of Hispania mounted on Quintilian's wall. "I doubt we can even make Brigantium in the time allotted, and, by the time we get all the way back down to Tarraco . . . " I followed the route, slowly, with my outstretched arm, for effect. It was clearly further from Calagguris than it had appeared on the map we had used in our planning sessions. There was no need to say anything more. It was obvious that we had to alter our plan, and "God just may be using Quintilian's neighbor to get our attention."

From where we stood, Paul called out, "Sir, uh, Señor Vitorius, where did you say you are to retrieve the vines?" Quintilian and Marcellus joined us, pleased to put to use the newly installed, very large, cowhide map of the region. Roman roads were painted indigo and labeled.

Marcellus pointed, "We are here, on the road from Calagurris to Pampaelo. We need only go a day's ride toward the coast, there, see? to Oiasso." Quintilian looked at us both, but held his tongue; the decision was Paul's alone. "I have my heart set on Brigantium." "But, Señor, it is a very long, dangerous road, over some very high mountain passes. How long did you say you have for this journey?" "We have to be back in Rome in fifteen . . ." I corrected him, "Fourteen." "Fourteen days." "Señor, this is not possible. Brigantium is six times the distance away from here, compared with the distance to Oiasso! Then you will need to get back to Caesaraugusta, then Tarraco. . . ." Marcellus trailed off. He could tell Paul was disappointed, but there is no arguing with such facts.

"I knew we should have kept to the main road." "Still, Brother," I interjected, "It was clearly God's will that we come spend this time with Quintilian." "Oh, my yes, of course it is." Quintilian had promised Paul to get him to Brigantium, so he felt obligated. "Look, gentlemen, as disappointing as it may be to not meet your goal, this is a much more realistic, and, dare I mention it, a more safe, goal. Why don't you make it easier on yourselves, go to the near shore, see what opportunities come your way. And it is a *beauuutiful* trip to Oiasso, I can attest to that!"

Paul paced a few steps, tapping his finger on his chin, rhythmically, then paced back to where we stood. I knew this posture. He was "pray/weighing" as I call it. He would pray as he weighed options, attempting to ascertain whatever inner mechanism he consulted in such situations, giving God time to impress upon him His will. But he never wasted much time waiting around for God to "speak to his heart." Paul was a man of action, and he was always in tune with the still, small voice, so he went with his instincts, assuming God would make it right. He was no enthusiast. And besides, there really was no option to weigh against going to the near shore. Brigantium was simply not practicable.

"Alright, then. Oiasso it is! I certainly see the wisdom in aiming for the closer shore. If we spend all our time, doggedly, attempting to reach Brigantium, when will we have time to spread the Word?" "Kind of defeats the real reason you came, eh?" Quintilian chuckled.

"I shall be glad of the company!" Marcellus exclaimed. "We leave at first light. Señor Fabius, I thank you for your hospitality. I will now go prepare." "You are welcome, sir. Thank you for assisting my friends. And, gentlemen, I still intend to help you meet your deadlines. I will have my fastest rig take you all the way back to Tarraco, when the time comes. There is *one* thing you need not worry about." Such a blessing! Paul and I were both speechless. In unison, spontaneously, we bowed in thanks.

We all lingered awhile on the veranda, digesting our midday meal making small talk, mostly about the road to Oiassa. I ticked off some of the more noteworthy bits of knowledge I had gleaned from the encyclopedia. Once we had stretched a bit, Quintilian proposed that we make the most of our remaining time. "Gentlemen," he said, "and I do hope you join us now, Luke, I propose that, since we've so little time remaining, we set right here, at this table, and conclude our dialectic." Since I had already admitted I had had my fill of reading the encyclopedia, I could no longer avoid the "talky talk" without raising eyebrows, so I stayed. But that was alright. I wished to show my gratitude to my host, and participating in his inquiry would be among the best ways to show him gratitude. He loved to talk about ideas!

"Good. Brother Paul, where did we leave off?" It pleased Paul to no end that Quintilian called him "brother."

P: That which is rightly called "rhetoric" must be crafted from truths, expressed beautifully, and must aim at the Good. Its complete opposite, namely, that which is false, ugly, and aims at evil, is rightly called bombast, or sophistry, or propaganda. But this sort of obviously ugly, evil communication one rarely encounters because it is self-defeating. If one's object is to lead others astray, or to influence attitudes for some unethical end, one obviously has to dress it up a bit, and at least give the appearance of truth, beauty and goodness. Otherwise, who would find that sort of discourse persuasive?

Q: Yes! "Beautiful lies" are no more beautiful than is an old prostitute hiding her hideousness behind too much make up.

P: I would say, "well put," but it is too repulsive an image for a man of refined sensibilities to grant affirmation!

We all laughed long and loud. The steward brought Rioja wine, well chilled, with much water, and sliced fruit mixed in. It was delicious and, according to Celsus, healthful!

So I raised my tankard and toasted, "to our health!" We had another good laugh.

Paul admitted he was still unconvinced that rhetoric was "ethical all the way done," as Quintilian put it.

Q: Let us take a few common sense instances, Paul. What does one call a physician whose malfeasance, let us call it "malpractice," leads to harm, injury and death as often as to health and well-being? Not "evil doctor," or "malpractitioner," or "ignorant doctor?"

L: A quack!

Q: Ha! Yes, and If he is given to botching surgeries, we might even call him a "butcher" (but this is an insult to the legitimate vocation of butcher).

Q: Again, what do we call it when a parent beats his or her child mercilessly? "Excessive discipline?" "Poor discipline?" "Discipline running amok?" No. It is called "abuse." Why? Because, in its perversity, and in its lack of grace and measure, by means of its very disproportion, it changes, in kind. And further, of that woman who victimizes her own child, (for the perversity is magnitudes worse in a woman than in a man, insofar as the woman is the "nurturer" of little ones) would it be proper to grant her the honorific, "mommy?" No. Terms of endearment are not properly applied to ones whose conduct violates the standards of decency and crosses into the realm of cruelty. Thus it is with rhetoric. One may refer to persuasive talk, in the broad sense, as "rhetoric," but, strictly speaking, because of its inherently ethical nature, that persuasive talk is rightly called "rhetoric" only which espouses truth, beauty and goodness.

P: Yes. This underscores the important relationship between dialectic and rhetoric; between wisdom and eloquence. Rhetoric, without a preceding dialectic, is dishonest and is no rhetoric, at all. If the materials from which the pleader builds his case are themselves flawed, the case is flawed.

Q: Indeed, and if the arguments are egregious enough, either on purpose or unintentionally, they warp the soul of the auditors. Plato would have none of this! It seems then, that, ideally, the regime of human faculties dictate that dialectic and rhetoric operate in tandem to ensure that one's oratory is both true and good.

P: And one's oratory is granted "Beauty" to the extent one's appeals to imagination are vivid, decorous, measured, and crafted according to the rules of art, as Aristotle says. Still, I worry that, if I utilize too many figures of speech, my language may seem pompous and arrogant. Doesn't one always run this risk when one embellishes ideas?

Q: Look, Paul, I will grant you, for the sake of argument that, in its barest instrumentality, rhetoric can be considered an amoral tool. But, scratch it just a little, and one exposes veins coursing with the red blood of truth-telling, of the establishment of trust, of dedication to beautiful, compelling language that directs the hearer toward The Good!

I had been thinking about Paul's reticence for some time, and so decided to try my hand at persuading him.

L: Paul, is it possible that your problem with rhetoric lies in your focus on homiletics over evangelism and apologia?

P: I have considered that, to be sure, Luke. Say on . . .

L: The degree of embellishment appropriate in homiletics is different than that apropos of deliberative discourse. When persuading on behalf of a course of action, one must muster the strongest imagery available (while observing standards of decorum). Such is not the case with a sermon. Because a sermon works, primarily, to affirm faith. Not as much vehemence, generally. (Where conviction of sin and conversion are the aim, perhaps a bit more vehemence is commendable.) I haven't studied rhetorical arts, but I think this makes sense. It all depends on whether your aim is to "contend for the faith" amongst fellow Believers, or to "win hearts and minds."

Q: Well said, Luke! In my own vocation, for example, one must continually bear in mind one's aim: 'am I out to secure justice for my client? Or to simply win the case?' One is a defensive posture, that has an abstract end in view. The other has as its primary aim the good of my neighbor.

L: I liked the point Quintilian made earlier, as well, namely, that it is complimentary to human beings to appeal both to head and to heart. Is the converse true, then? That it is, therefore, a diminution of human nature to make purely logical appeals?

P: Certainly not!

Q: It most certainly is! If human beings were pure minds, maybe. But we have emotions, and minds, and wills, and appetites.

One could see, once again, Paul was having an epiphany. He re-directed the disputatio to something that had been on his mind since we met Quintilian, eight days ago.

P: Now, when you ascribe so much importance to this "vir bonum" the so-called "good man," do you intend . . .

Q: Not "so-called," he must be both a good man, and well spoken. His goodness must be established.

P: What is the basis of his goodness, and at what does it aim?

Q: His goodness is the fruit of his striving after personal virtue and its aim is, ultimately, to serve the demos with integrity and good judgment. A bad man cannot exercise good judgment because his rule is bent, as it were.

P: I see. So you wish to build a virtuous society by means of virtuous leaders?

Q: Precisely. This is the end of rhetoric and the end of politics. This is, in fact, where politics and rhetoric merge.

P: But what of religion?

Q: What of it?

P: One would think the virtue sought would, in some way, benefit from or be influenced by belief in the gods? It is a bit naïve to assume you can find these good men to lead you.

Q: Of course. Of course, Paul, you would have an interest in taking the dialectic in this direction. Well, it may surprise you, but I agree with you on this point. Belief in the gods, especially in Jove, plays a key role in the development of virtue and of character. The lessons learned from their conduct, from their foibles, are an indispensable feature of religion in this process.

L: I was just thinking that there are significant implications for rhetorical doctrine in what you say. For example, rhetoric can be understood as speaking the truth to one's neighbor, for his betterment.

P: Yes . . . and we established that figures of speech help build both beautiful imagery and strong rhythm. The canon of style is about introducing to one's argumentation both poetry and aesthetics. It's about speaking with truth with beauty and grace, which adds impulse to the Truth.

Rhetoric, in the final analysis, moves the soul toward the Good. Our preachers need to, as you say, Quintilian, use language masterfully to "pique the imagination, which stirs the emotions, which moves the soul."

Q: Yes. Paul, you've got it!

P: We determined that, if one's argument is potent enough, and the audience will supply a little imagination, one can be transported through the use of metaphor. We further concluded that the act of appealing to the audience's imagination is complimentary to their humanity; it cultivates in them moral imagination and aesthetic sensibilities. But this power must be wielded with grace, decorum, propriety, proportion and measure, so, even when it comes to the fanciful dimensions of rhetoric, good judgment is cultivated.

L: In sum, mastering rhetoric can teach one to *be* Good but also, to *aim at* The Good. The former entails the goodness cultivated within the rhetor (virtue); the latter, the Goodness to which our rhetoric points (but also, in a deeper sense, *from* which our rhetoric points!).

Q: You've been listening, after all, Luke!

P: And, is it not also the case, Quintilian, that since, as Aristotle teaches, trust is essential to persuasion, since no reasonable man would allow himself to be persuaded by one whose word cannot be trusted?

Q: I believe this, yes.

P: So, again, the cultivation of trustworthiness is part of the process of cultivating excellence in rhetorical arts. As you helped us see, Quintilian, skill in rhetoric entails character development, as well as wisdom and eloquence. I appreciate this view of the subject, and I will tell you this: rhetoric conceived in this way is complementary to the Christian life in many ways!

Q: I am happy to hear that you will find it useful. (It was the most cordial reply Quintilian could come up with, in the moment.) Here is my doctrine, in a nutshell: The orator must be a good man because he is educated to lead and a leader cannot create civic virtue, through good laws, and by praising virtue, if *he has not cultivated virtue himself*, or if his judgment is warped. To speak credibly on affairs of state, the speaker must be credible, and love both the state and its citizens. This is why I maintain that, in a society of freedmen, liberal arts education, with its emphasis on the twin faculties of dialectic and rhetoric, is indispensable.

P: This makes imminent sense! And one is reminded that Plato's prescription for "redeeming" rhetoric, elucidated in the conclusion of his *Phaedrus*, entails a methodology grounded in the study of the soul. I think Aristotle took seriously Plato's suggestion, so, in his treatise on rhetoric, he makes "ethos" (personal character) one of the three "modes of artistic proof."

Q: Yes, which is why, later, Aristotle asserts, of ethos, that a trustworthy character is one of the requisites of persuading because "We believe good men more fully and more readily than others: this is true generally whatever the question is, and absolutely true where exact certainty is impossible and opinions are divided." In fact, he considers character the most effective means of persuasion the rhetor possesses.

L: You have that memorized? Impressive! And I must say, gentlemen, I find impressive this entire portrait you are now painting. I, for the life of me, do not understand why everybody is not required, by law, to study these things. I should think it would be in the state's interest to have citizens educated for liberty in precisely the manner you indicate!

Paul stood up and started pacing. He was on fire.

P: Yes, Luke, it is important to raise up good citizens. But I am excited by the potential for the church of rhetoric so conceived. I was just thinking about my early education, and it came to me how, later on, Aristotle further identifies *phronesis* with ethos. This is a key extension because phronesis is exercised with respect to the other; the neighbor. Plato's negative view of the Sophists was motivated by his conviction that their distortions would warp the soul of Athenians. The more I ponder these things the more clearly I see how rhetoric cultivates in the orator, good character, and in the auditors, as well, because it is all about the proper moving of the soul. This gets to the heart of what rhetoric is about; how it plays a part in human excellence.

L: And this clarifies for me why rhetoric has long been considered the capstone of the liberal arts.

P: And, when we last spoke of my attempt to reach my kinsmen, Quintilian, I could not stop thinking about the close tie between cultivating imagination, and the value of education in rhetoric to a sacramental view of life; to nourishing souls that are receptive to spiritual truths.

L: "Ears to hear and eyes to see . . . "

P: Exactly! Proper movement of the soul, and proper "alignment," involves reason, but also, memory, imagination, emotions, and will." Hearts and minds.

Q: Well, my friend, you have certainly appropriated every jot and tittle of our conversations for advancement of your cause! Ha!

P: Rhetoric is a tuning fork of the soul. It "rightly turns" the soul so that we are in harmony with the True, the Good, and the Beautiful. We learn to appreciate what we ought and to avoid what we ought. This is the function of no other art. To be sure, rhetoric does not function properly without dialectic. The two are "antistrophes" one of another, as Aristotle says. They are like two plants that grow side-by-side. Above ground, they seem like separate plants, though of the same variety; below the ground, one discovers as he tugs a little, they share a common root!

Quintilian asked why we had employed no scribe to write this down? "I will call my man." I told him not to worry, that I'd take care of it. "Shouldn't you be jotting down notes, at least?" "No. I am fine." I tapped my temple and winked. "Oh! I see," Quintilian was impressed.

P: Now, Quintilian, please do not take offence at what I am about to say. I cannot help but work out the ramifications for the Christian church of all that has been said. I do not wish to offend, but time is short, and I am inspired now, so I need to talk through. . . .

Q: Please, friend. You do not have to explain yourself to me.

P: Rhetoric is involved with the Word. But HOW? Introducing movement toward the Good; to embrace the Truth established by dialectic. It motivates; it is an order of desire.

Q: Yes! Just like in *The Phaedrus*? with the lover and the non-lover and the base lover.

P: Have you ever made conversation with one who is so concerned with abstract truth you wonder if he has any affection for "the other?" Not only that, I have met men whose only allegiance is to self. It is as though he never developed bonds with others, with his neighbors, family, even. This matter of cultivating proper sentiments . . . Paul snapped his fingers. One sense of the "well-ordered soul" is to love that which is lovely; to care about what one ought to care about, it clarifies the motion of the soul, so to speak! Do you see?

Both Quintilian and I nodded in unison. Divine wisdom was palpable, and it was sweet.

P: Friends, I understand now the very deep and abiding relationship between rhetoric and the love of God. It draws the soul toward the Good, toward God. It is intimately involved with proper motion; with the ordering of the soul. It gives impulse to the Truth by adorning ideas, making them beautiful and appealing; compelling! Luke, in the gospel we preach Jesus is associated with two things, above all else: Love and Logos. God is Love and Jesus is the Logos, the Word. Insofar as the mind is drawn to heavenly truth, through the Logos, and rhetoric, according to Aristotle, is constituted of Ethos, Pathos, and Logos, rhetoric is the *intellectual* love of God!

Q: I have never even considered . . .

We were all treated to direct revelation knowledge. We drank deeply! The sun was starting to go down now. Nobody noticed when the servants came and lit torches.

P: When I ponder how the mysteries of God are cast in allegory and figuration, that they are accessed through imagination, I cannot help, now thanks to Quintilian, here, but see the role of rhetoric in analogical thinking! Our truths are often told by parable, some perhaps discoverable only by parable. One would surely expect Jesus, who came to this world to show us the Father, to speak plainly; to use clear logic. And yet, he spoke almost exclusively in parables. This is very telling. Could it be that rhetoric is itself implicated in unlocking the very riches of God's grace? This possibility took Paul's breath away. He physically contracted into himself, exhaled and said. "Well, friends, I am spent. I perceive the inspiration has passed. As Socrates might say, 'I am no longer speaking in dithyrambs!' I need some sleep. Quintilian, I can't even begin. . . ."

Q: "The feeling is mutual, my friend. Sleep well."

Paul walked away, still savoring the twilight, "I will go to the shore of the known world tomorrow, then, I am ready to return to Rome and meet my Maker. My race is run. The finish-line is within sight." Quintilian turned to me and said, "That is a great metaphor! Tell him he should use it." "He already has," I said.

Paul and I walked the grounds, praying and counting our blessings. We prayed earnestly for Quintilian's conversion. As the unusually radiant moon rose out of the orange, rocky crags into the cobalt evening sky, we stopped to watch a family of deer drink from a spring. They bounded away toward the river, we thanked God for his protection, for his provision, and for the many blessings since our departure from Ostia. Our time with Quintilian was turning out to be among the greatest of blessings. "Brother," I asked Paul, "would you ever expect God to grant such a powerful connection to such a learned chap, in such a remote wilderness?" "No. Then again: God's thoughts are *not* our thoughts, and His ways are not our ways!" "This is a good thing."

13

To the Far Shore and Back Again

MARCELLUS WAS NOT ONE to tarry long where there was work to be done. We just finished breakfast when he stormed up the road to the villa, jumped out of his cart, spread his arms wide and boomed, "Come gentlemen! Daylight is wasting." "Ha!" Paul popped a grape in his mouth and said, in his high-pitched, morning voice, "Are you serious, friend? Look!" he positively crowed, pointing, "The moon is still well up in the sky!" Marcellus laughed as he grabbed a plate and sat down.

We collected a few things and took off for the coast as soon as we finished the last of the sausages and drained the tea pot. Quintilian had not joined us. Apparently he had risen early to go inspect the mine and check on the progress of the olive oil production he and his neighbor had been planning. "Busy man." "He loves it," says Marcellus. "Most ambitious man I know." "So it seems," said Paul.

Oiasso, is a small port city directly north of Calagguris, a short day's ride, not far from Pampaelo. "There is a new road, just built last year, the Ab Asturica Burdigalam," Marcellus was proud of the progress in his land, "runs right through Oiasso." Paul mentioned, later, out of earshot of Marcellus, so as not to give offence, how pleased he was that all these new roads were built, seemingly, just to accommodate our mission work. It *was* quite a coincidence. So, we crossed the Iberus and rode north to Pampaelo, then made a quick jog over to Oiasso. The grapevines were stored in a barn somewhere on the Burdigala side of town. Marcellus dropped us off at an inn, not far from the docks, and asked us to procure rooms. He thought he would have just enough time to find the place, load the grapevines, and return to the inn before it got too dark. "Would it not be better to leave them in the trader's care until morning?" asked Paul. "Wouldn't they be more secure? I should think thieves might bother your cart if it were—" Marcellus, who had been stretching his neck and back, giving his bottom a rest, jumped back up in the driver's seat. "I'm not worried about that. And we need to leave at first light . . . " he prompted the team and was off, " . . . moon or no!"

We got two rooms, then went to look for a bite to eat. As the sun set, in a brilliant mélange of fiery orange, pink, gold that shone like God's filigree in the tapestry of the evening sky, we (Paul, a young couple we had met, who were followers of the Way, and yours truly,) found a nearby spot, out of the way, where we could sing our evening devotion. Some gulls joined us, from a distance. A pelican landed nearby. Paul told an allegory about how the mother pelican, when food is scarce, will pierce her own breast to give of her own blood to nourish and sustain her young. "If that isn't a type of Christ," Paul exclaimed, "I don't know what is!" We all agreed.

Paul allowed himself a rare moment of satisfaction, but there were no others around, so we decided to walk back toward the docks, then entered the market square, just in time to overhear a little, stooped woman, packing up her food cart, chanting to herself a Psalm. We startled her, at first, but when she ascertained the nature of our business, and that we meant her no harm, she welcomed us to the end of the earth and offered us her leftovers. We thanked her much and, as we ate, shared the gospel with her. She had family whom she wished us to meet. We left word at the inn and followed her home, taking turns relieving her of the burden of pushing her cart (thereby cutting in half the time it took to get to her little shack). We passed a lovely evening with the woman and her children (the father was out to sea). They were eager to hear the gospel, but, having heard, they seemed disinclined to act upon the word, only thanking us, politely, then hinting that it was time for them to retire. We, ourselves, had an early morning and a long day's ride ahead of us, so we prayed a quick prayer and returned to the inn.

Next morning, we left as soon as we had downed the scant breakfast provided by the innkeeper. I think Marcellus gave us all of 3 minutes to eat. He, of course, had eaten his fill before we had ever risen. "Slept like a baby. Let's go. Daylight is wasting." It did *no* good telling him it was not yet daylight! "My goodness, Marcellus!" Paul whistled. "Those are, without doubt, the finest grapevines I have ever seen." "Yes, they are beautiful! I can hardly wait to plant them! They will have the full summer ahead of them, to get established. I trust your time on the coast was fruitful?"

Paul recounted a little of our exploits. "This hunched over lady," Marcellus asks, "was she maybe a little taller than those wheels? Wore a scarf on her head? Sold mostly bread and cheese in her cart?" We nodded. "Did she live about 15 minutes' walk north of the docks? "That she did!" I replied. "Ha! Chances are that was my mum's auntie. Did she have her three children living with her in a little shack, said her husband was 'out to sea'? "Aye," we both replied, in unison. "That's her. What did she try to sell you? "Nothing," said Paul. "In fact, she fed us what little she had that did not sell, then we went home with her to share the gospel with her children." "Share the what?"

"The Gospel," said Paul, "Good News." "Oh, that! Right. You are referring to the stories about that Jew, the one from Galilee, er Jesus? Yes?" "Yes." Paul did a gloss of his preaching, both what he'd said last evening on the docks and in the auntie's home, in Oiasso and even incorporated into the homily the best of his gems from our three days in Ostia. Now that his letter to the Hebrews was mostly finished, one could hear elements of that work emerging, fully, in Paul's preaching. Marcellus seemed rather interested.

Eventually, not far out of Pampaelo, the topic of conversation shifted, much to my discomfort, to the topic of my needing, in Paul's estimation, to write a witness to the Work and Words of Jesus. "I don't know, brother. I have so much happening in my life, and I—"

"Brother Luke, writing is a talent God has given you. Your capacity for recalling detail is astonishing! Mark did a fine job, and what he did will be a supreme blessing to the church, but your perspective, I think, will be a valuable complement to Mark's witness. Please pray about it."

"Well, my brother, I thank you, and, yes, I will pray about it. But I tell you now, I would be much more interested in chronicling *our* exploits! It has been a pleasure serving beside you and, my, what we have seen, and what you have suffered in the Name—"

"Yes, yes. I knew what I was getting into, friend. The spirit of Christ impressed on me, from that very first encounter, that I would suffer for this Gospel even as I had caused so much suffering."

Luke was simultaneously recollecting the various times Paul had been shipwrecked, stoned, left for dead, and arrested, and making mental notes regarding potential anecdotes for his history of Paul's missionary journeys.

"One caveat, friend. Regarding our most recent activity, we must exercise utmost discretion so as not to endanger those who will serve as leaders within the congregations we launch."

"Ummhmm."

The mere mention of the gravity of the situation elicited assent. The dangers grew daily.

" . . . of course God will grant them protection, but Nero's wrath seems to grow more severe each day. He is intent on killing us all. We must act accordingly. I do not foresee this rancor abating any time soon."

"Of course, you are correct, Brother Paul. Alas."

"So, please do write a witness, but, yes, don't get anyone killed!"

"Seems to me the churches in Hispania Tarraconensis and Gaul will be particularly vulnerable, since resistance to Nero seems to be arising primarily from these quarters."

"Yes. Nero will no doubt blame the Christians."

We stopped in Pampaelo for a quick bite, then set out for the villa. As we ate, Marcellus asked more questions, so we discussed the things of God all the way back. By the time we rounded the bend, and dropped down the little arroyo into Calagurritanum, Marcellus was converted. We were grooming the horses and making plans for his family to be baptized when we learned from Africanus that Quintilian was no longer at the villa. Apparently he had left for Nova Carthago where, according to the overseer, he was to join Galba's retinue, bound for Rome. At this news, Marcellus exclaimed, "I *knew* it! That explains all the activity; wagons coming and going. Horsemen at all hours."

Paul simply nodded, with a knowing glance. Africanus said the master had made arrangements to get us back to Tarraco, and that we were welcome to enjoy the villa as long as was required to refresh ourselves. "How very generous," I said, then excused myself to go freshen up a bit and asked Africanus if the encyclopedia were still in the great room? "No, sir," he replied. "We moved it to the library." "May I?" "Of course! In fact, Master Quintilian had us place some writing materials there, for your convenience." "Gentlemen, you know where to find me," I intended to make full use of Quintilian's hospitality.

"Luke," Paul called out, "before you dive into that medical encyclopedia again, how much time do you think we have to spare?" "Well, let us see," I had to think, "tomorrow will be day fourteen, yes?" "I believe so, yes." "I should think we ought to allow ourselves one day to rest up—" " . . . then we head to Caesaraugusta." Paul finished my sentence. Paul also, discreetly, made the "sign of the cross," meaning we also needed to get Marcellus's family baptized. We both nodded agreement and I was off to my library, Paul to his room, to rest and write. It had been a whirlwind trip to the end of the earth and back!

14

Harvest Time in Caesaraugusta

WE HADN'T BEEN ABLE to arrange for a family baptism at Marcellus' villa. It was just too far in the wrong direction, and he was occupied with the new grapes. They needed to be put in the ground *post haste*. We decided we could send Apollos and Timothy back to Burdigala by way of Calagguris. So zealous a man as Marcellus would likely, by the time the brethren finished up in Tarraco and Caesaraugusta, have a flock all prepared to receive instruction in the faith! The extra distance would be well worth it.

When we pulled up to the inn, on the west end of town, not far from the Emporion, it was evening of Day 19. We had only one full day to join up with Team Alpha (if Clement had succeeded in his mission,) spend a day teaching the new converts, hold a baptism, then leave for Tarraco. We had ridden hard and still had a long road ahead, not to mention the sail across the Great Sea, back to Ostia. We sought privacy in a grove of elms, a short walk over a knob, behind the inn, and sang Evening Prayers, washed off the dust, then turned in. I dreamt of breakfasting at that cute little café across from the Forum!

And that is where we headed, first thing in the morning. No time to waste! We were enjoying our morning tea, waiting on our fruit, nuts and boiled grains when, across the way, popping out of the Provincial Court, we recognized Maximus! "There's a familiar face," Paul shouted! "Good morning!"

"Good morning, gentlemen!" Maximus walked up to us, smiling. "Welcome back to our humble market!" "It is good to be back," said Paul. "And I am so pleased you are the first person we have met whom we recognize!"

"I would love to join you, but I've been asked to run an urgent errand. You say 'first person,' does that mean you've not yet seen Prosperus? or Zenas?" "That is correct." "Don't go anywhere! I know where they are; it is right on the way to where I am bound. I'll send them to you, and then I would love to join you when I've taken care of my responsibility."

"Absolutely. Terrific idea," says I.

"Or will you be preaching in the same location most of this day?"

"No time for that, actually. We just need to touch base with Zenas, check on his progress, then do some teaching, and head back to Tarraco on the morrow."

Maximus absolutely lit up when we mentioned teaching.

"Good! I shall be there," he shot us a "glance." "I have good news. Will we baptize new members tomorrow?" "Yes." He turned and ran off down the alley, in the direction of The Prætorium, before we could discern the nature of his good news, but I had a hunch Zenas had had good success with the young man! Between sips of tea, as we sat in silence, awaiting the arrival of the youngsters, Paul said, "Zenas certainly has a way with the youth."

In a short while, as we finished our breakfast, Xanthippe, Probus, Zenas, and Prosperus all joined us. "Where is young Polyxene?" Paul asked, innocently enough. Xanthippe controlled herself just long enough to blurt out, "I don't know!" Probus consoled the poor girl. We were shocked. Apparently, Xanthippe had prevailed on Diocles to allow them to stay with a Christian family in town while he road ahead to Toletum, to confirm whether uncle was ready to receive them. Meantime, the girls went to the market unescorted, three days prior, and Xanthippe had lost track of her younger sister. She disappeared, and Xanthippe had been searching for her ever since. When the gravity of Polyxene's situation had sunk in, we all bowed our heads, right there at our table, and prayed earnestly that our Heavenly Father would send His holy angel to protect the young girl from all harm and danger, and return her to her sister, that He would grant her mercy to avoid whatever evil the Devil had in mind for her.[1] Xanthippe was much comforted, but still, understandably distraught.

---

1. Xanthippe and Polyxene, are commemorated in the Greek Orthodox Church on September 23. According to an apocryphal book that bears their names, Xanthippe converted her husband, Probus, to the Christian faith; Polyxene, was kidnapped, spirited away from Spain, to Achaia in Greece, and, according to legend, was baptized by St. Andrew. "St. Xanthippe and St. Polyxene, Disciples of the Apostles," http://www.antiochian.org/node/16749 (accessed 17 Oct 2016).

"Brother Paul! Brother Luke! Friends!" Clement, Timothy, Onesimus, and Apollos all walked up as we sat in stunned silence. We moved to a larger table, off to the side of the establishment this time, so we could talk a little more privately. Apollos ordered a feast that fed the whole table. (Apparently he had charmed someone ought of a few drachma. Once a showman, always a showman. No denying, though, it *was* delicious! (I should not bite the hand that, literally feeds me! I'm sure the wo-, er, person, who gave the drachmæ, gave it "unto the Lord.") Paul pulled Apollos aside, after dinner, presumably to ask forgiveness for the outburst on the boat. Everyone knew about it.

We shared the bad news of Polyxene's disappearance, and then, more for Xanthippe's benefit than anything, I asked the three members of "Team Alpha" to tell us all the good news of their travels along the Via Aquitania then down to Caesaraugusta. "Clement, how was your adventure since we last set foot in this market, let's see," Paul ciphered on his fingers, "um, 11 days ago? Did you find them right away? Did you have any trouble? You must be exhausted!"

Clement told us all about how he had had a little trouble in the mountains, to the East, between Hispania and Gaul, but that God had watched out for him. And, yes, he had met up with the brethren right away, because they were in the main marketplace of Burdigala, as expected. "I could have asked about anyone on the street, though, and found them! They were the talk of the town!" "Yes, let me guess," quipped Paul, "Apollos' eloquence was a huge draw!?" Apollos blushed. Timothy asked, in jest, "However did you guess, Brother Paul!" The levity was much needed. We ate and talked, talked and ate. God had obviously blessed our efforts in Burdigala, as he had in each and every stop we had made. It would be most interesting to hear from "Team Gamma," who'd travelled along the coastal highway, the "Via Herculea." If they had experienced success as great as ours, then this would be marked among our most successful, least perilous, missionary trips ever. Apparently there were converts in Gaul, as well as some who had already believed, but had not been instructed. Apollos, Timothy, and Onesimus were anxious to return and "work the harvest." We were anxious to return Timothy and Onesimus to them.

"What happened to Brigantium?" Onesimus was incredulous when we recounted our change of plan, and our visit to Quintilian's family estate. "True, Brother Onesimus," Paul replied, "I have dreamed of nothing more than taking the gospel to the far shore of the world for a long, long time.

But we made it to Oiasso, so I am satisfied. We made the coast, thanks be to God!" God used us, not in the manner we had hoped, but I can see how God has worked to strategically place men all through Southern Gaul *and* Hispania Tarraconensis *and* Baetica, to establish His Kingdom all through Hispania!" All agreed. All gave thanks. All prayed for further success.

We sent word, through Xanthippe, Probus, Zenas, and Prosperus, to all who wished to learn more about The Way, to meet us on the piazza beside the marketplace after the close of business, for intensive teaching, and that there would be a baptismal service in the morning, before we took to the road. (We did not disclose that location. To do so would have been unwise.) At the end of our meeting, later in the evening, much later, it would be evident who was genuinely interested and who was there to spy on us. The spies would never find out where the baptismal rite was to be performed. If they did show up at the river, they were likely to get dunked . . . against their will!"

By morning Zenas let Paul and me know that he had prevailed on Apollos and Timothy, to remain in Caesaraugusta and work with Xanthippe, Probus, Maximus, and the rest of the church that was quickly forming. We deemed this acceptable, because, experience had shown that the quicker we ordained leaders, then left them to work out for themselves, how best to apply the teachings to their particular customs, their social *ethos*, and their peculiar religious sensibilities, the more indigenous leaders would arise and take charge. Then it was important that we re-visit from time to time, maintain correspondence, and establish oversight to keep them on the narrow path, so to speak. We all agreed it would take until mid-summer, to establish a base in Caesaraugusta then Apollos, Timothy, and Onesimus would spend some time in Burdigala, and winter in Narbo. It seemed good to us that, while in Narbo, they could pray for the Spirit's guidance and see what field God would have them harvest next. Paul gave his blessing, asking only that they, "please, return to Burdigala by way of Calagurris, so you can check on our new brother, Marcellus."

"He is the one who drove us to the coast, to Oiasso, to get his grapes," I interjected. "Oh. Right." "Yes, and Marcellus will no doubt know some families in and around Oiasso who would— Well, bless my soul!" Dear reader, whom do you imagine appeared at that very moment!? "Brother Marcellus Vitorius! What are *you* doing in Caesaraugusta!? Friends, this is the very man of whom I *just* spoke." Nods and smiles and handshakes all around. Paul continued, "Marcellus, whom do you know around Oiasso who would, first, be open to the gospel of Jesus Christ, and, second, who would have commerce in Burdigala?" Paul was thinking that, if we could locate people who made regular trips to Burdigala, The Word would spread more quickly, and that ties would be built between churches in the two communities, and villages in between. News travelled abroad by sailing ship in proportions geometrically greater than any other means, so port cities were always prime targets. Marcellus had, not only a long list of folks he knew on the coast, but he assured us he had been spreading the Good News in and around Calagguris. "Apollos and Timothy, I can guarantee you a large crowd in Calagguris." We made a few plans for their return, but Marcellus quickly changed the course of the conversation to that which prompted his hasty journey to Caesaraugusta.

"I am all alone in this new faith," Marcellus lamented. "I have so many questions, and no one of whom I may ask them! I thought up an excuse to come down to Caesaraugusta, hoping to have a little more time with you before you return to Rome!" His simple sincerity touched us all. Paul replied, "We are at your disposal, Señor Vitorius. We do not have to leave for Tarraco until tomorrow morning!" I nodded and smiled assent. Eventually we ascertained that what Marcellus needed most was instruction in prayer. We taught him the Prayer Jesus Taught, the Creed, and this (something we were just working up, to build and bolster the image of God's spotless Lamb. Paul explained, the leader chants thus: "Lamb of God you take away the sin of the world" and the response is: "have mercy on us." Then, inverting the phrase, "Have mercy on us, O Lamb of God" and, variation on the theme, "Grant us peace . . . " repeated once for effect, "Grant us peace." Dropping the octave brings closure. You see? "I love chant! My family did this style at our family altar when I was a boy." "It *is* lovely; it builds unity between leader and people," Paul opined. Marcellus enthusiastically seconded. "Yes. Will you help me commit it to memory?" So we repeated thrice, without interruption,

> Lamb of God you take away the sin of the world,
> Have mercy on us.
> Have mercy on us, O Lamb of God.
> Grant us peace. Grant us peace.

"What elegant simplicity. What lovely symmetry. Thank you. Thank you!"

"Now, each morning, before I open my eyes, my practice" Paul continued the lesson, "is to make the sign of the cross, to remember my baptism, recite the Prayer of Our Lord and the creed, which is a pithy profession of the faith we believe, teach, and confess. I rise and chant a psalm or hymn. When I am with others, I will often do some sort of call and response, like this 'Agnus Dei.'" "Thank you. This is why I sought you out!" Marcellus' trip was not in vain. "This is very helpful. But I have not been baptized." The Holy Spirit was drawing this one. "Ha! Well, young man, before we leave for Tarraco, in the morning, we plan to baptize all who have received instruction and who seem ready. If you can stay, and will receive a few more hours of instruction in the faith this evening . . . " Marcellus did not wait for Paul to finish! "Yes! This is the most important thing in my life. I want to believe. This is what I am after!"

"I will work with him," Zenas volunteered because he was already working with the young lawyers and their friends and family in Caesaraugusta who had demonstrated their desire to join our number. "Please teach him all the prayers and devotions I just mentioned, won't you, brother?" "Of course," said Zenas. I was compiling in my mind a "grammar" of devotional and catechetical items to utilize that evening, as we prepared novices for the baptismal rite. "I think, perhaps, it would be fruitful to lead with prayers and devotional elements, especially the Prayer of our Lord, and teach the faith with reference to these 'chief elements.'" Paul nodded and said, "Brilliant! Do that. Maybe you could briefly touch on the difference between the Old and New Covenants?" "Certainly. And I could introduce that instruction by reviewing the Commandments." Paul saw the beauty of it. "Terrific idea! Should be able to do all this in three or four hours. Please implement it with the others. Oh! And have them memorize the words Jesus spoke when he instituted the Holy Supper." And so Caesaraugusta became the first place we practiced this methodical, pithy, grammar of the true faith. Before that day, instruction in the faith was much less formalized, or "codified," so to speak. So, the approach I used with my new converts, the remainder of my life, point of fact, was born of necessity. We had so little time to work with these lambs. Life-giving instruction was borne out of Paul's impending death. I appreciated both the tragedy, and the blessing, of our new procedure.

As the crowd gathered for our afternoon session, and Paul had Timothy to himself, he pulled Timothy aside and asked if he had had any problems with Apollos. "No, none at all. Well, maybe he got a little long-winded on a couple occasions, but we worked out a signal . . . whenever I pointed toward the ground," folding his arms, then looking down and bending the

wrist of his free hand and pointing, subtly, with his forefinger, then looking up and cradling his chin between that forefinger and thumb, so as to
disguise the gesture, "he toned down his rhetoric immediately. The trick is
to get eye contact with Apollos!" We laughed. Paul did not.

We broke for supper and invited any who wished to prepare to be
baptized early the next morning to return in two hours. Now that the crowd
had thinned we got serious, broke into groups of four or five, led by Paul,
Zenas, Timothy, Onesimus, and myself. Paul made sure Prosperus was in
his group. He wished to disciple this young man himself, and Zenas asked to
work with Maximus, Xanthippe, and Probus. God had granted them strong
bonds of love in the ten days they had spent nearly every hour together.

Sometime, around the middle of the night, Paul approached me about
Prosperus. "I think it would be good for Prosperus to ride along with us to
Tarraco." "Okay," I said. "Do you have plans for him?" Space was at a premium. When we left Quintilian's, we had not anticipated needing the larger
"freighter wagon," but selected a smaller, more durable and faster, horse
cart. Even a single additional passenger, with belongings, would make the
trip significantly less comfortable. "He tells me he has business in Tarraco,
anyway, and I would like extra time with him. He is an extraordinarily
bright young man, very earnest, and I believe God may have big plans for
him." "Well, if that is what's needed, who am I to question it?" Paul smiled.
"He is ready for 'strong meat'! Ha! I get the impression he is already dis-
satisfied with the pure milk of the Word." I hope he is prepared for a painful
backbone and a sore backside.

Paul taught him the entire way. He also got down to fundamental, life
questions, with Quintilian's apprentice. Paul urged him to change direction, with his parents' consent, of course, and seek ordination. "You have
been given ample gifts in keeping with the holy ministry, my son." Paul
was serious about the things of God, and he was very persuasive when he
was recruiting someone to leadership. "I can see you will distinguishing
yourself as a teacher and a preacher. Rarely have I seen one with so strong
an appetite for the things of God." But Prosperus was torn. It was a great
honor to apprentice under Marcus Fabius Quintilianus. Not only he, but his
parents, had sacrificed a great deal to "enter that gate. He was already well
down the path to fame and fortune." At any rate, Prosperus prayed about
and weighed his decision all the way to Tarraco.

Back in Caesaraugusta, just before we set out for Tarraco, at first
light, after we all—all twenty of the souls gathered—recited together the

seven elements we taught and memorized into the wee hours of the previous night (the "three hours" would have worked quite well, *if* nobody asked a question!) Paul led us in the prayers we had memorized, blessed them, and after Apollos led us in a hymn (his contribution was limited; circumscribed, rather,) Twelve souls were baptized as the sun arose, on our third day. Among these were Prosperus, Probus, *and* Maximus (yes, Zenas stayed up all one night with Maximus, a week before. By morning he was exhausted, but born again!) Xanthippe's brother, Diocles, had come for her and they were probably already on the road back to Toletum by now, so her baptism would have to wait a little longer. (Diocles was so tired and angry when he arrived, she could not disclose the bad news about Polyxene, so she made up something about her having gone to the country with a relative of the family with whom they stayed, to help pick berries or something. He said he could not spare the two days for her to return, so he would pick her up the next time he was in town. His uncle had put him right to work running freight.) After we sang a farewell hymn and the brethren prayed over us, they sent us down the road to Tarraco.

15

End Game

It is Day Twenty-four. The ship sails for Rome tomorrow. Zenas, Paul, Clement, Epaphras, and I will return to Ostia, stop at Lucina's for a quick meal and a brief accounting of our time in Hispania, then we will return Paul to his jailer in Rome "before sundown on Day Thirty, Maius 15." Clement returned with us to relieve his parents from worry. Epaphras has to tend his fields. We decided Epaphras should get back home and not serve as one who stayed behind to teach, baptize, and ordain leaders.

Before Barnabas and Aristarchus had even had a chance to shake the dust from their garments, Paul asked for a report regarding developments in Astigi. Barnabas replied that they had travelled a long, long distance down the Via Herculea but that they had become so busy with the harvest in Nova Carthago they decided to stay there, then return after the gathering in Tarraco, and press on to Astigi at that time. "The Via Herculea between Nova Carthago and Baetica is much more difficult than that going *to* Nova Carthago, from Tarraco, through Valentia, down the coast." "Here come the excuses." Sometimes, Brother Paul can be such a . . . , I thought to myself. Barnabas ignored him. "Astigi is deep in the interior of Hispania Baetica. I was told it is a howling wilderness, and urged, because, beyond Nova Carthago it is so perilous, to man and beast, because of the mountains and the thieves, we were advised to not attempt a crossing until summer." "I see," said Paul. "We were told it takes much longer to get to Astigi than one would expect, looking at the map. So, since God's Spirit was so manifestly at work in Nova Carthago. . . ." "Yes, well, thanks be to God you are both here with us now." Barnabas pointed out to Paul that it was a miracle they managed four whole days in Nova Carthago. Paul hugged them and sent them off to get cleaned up. He asked them to return by Evening Prayers, so he could include them in the equipping of the new converts.

Not wanting to disappoint, as he walked off, Barnabas assured Paul that, since he was staying behind, he would definitely fulfill the great apostle's promise to Hierotheus. Paul was overjoyed to hear from him that Hierotheus had, in fact, sent word that he would arrive in Tarraco in a few days.

Onesimus, upon learning that Hierotheus was coming, begged to stay in Tarraco just long enough to greet his old chum, whom he had not seen for years, since they were lads in Achaia. He was granted permission, as long as he would promise to then race up to Caesaraugusta, with Prosperus. Prosperus announced, a few hours after our arrival in Tarraco, his decision to no longer work for Quintilian (whom he secretly suspected would never again set foot in Hispania Tarraconensis). "I have decided," he declared, "to accept Brother Paul's kind offer, to enter fulltime pastoral ministry.[1] Something tells me my master has gone to Rome, probably for good. It will be an even greater honor to have apprenticed under Brother Paul and to spend my life in service to the Living God." All were pleased with his decision, saw the wisdom in it, and gave glory to God.

Paul, in front of everyone, instructed Onesimus that Prosperus' apprenticeship as deacon was to begin immediately upon his arrival back in Caesaraugusta, that Onesimus was to tell Timothy to prepare Prosperus for the work of the ministry, taking him, at least, to Burdigala, then, when he was ready, to send him to Tarraco to serve as pastor of a church to be established there among the learned class of the Provincial Capital. So, Prosperus concluded his affairs in Tarraco, which he expected would take at least two days, which coincided with Onesimus' desire to reunite with Heirotheus. All things work together for good.

Paul had his own item of business for Onesimus. "Could you please relay to Timothy this message: Tell him I would like him to pray about finding me in Syrian Antioch, at Manæn's place, where I have rooms. If I should happen to be released permanently, that is where he will find me, or, if I am not there, I will leave word with Manæn. "Ahem," I interrupted. Paul sniggered. "Well, brother, I guess I assumed. . . . If I am not there, I will likely be at Luke's then." When Paul was in *my* home town it was a given, he

---

1. According to an 8th-century Spanish tradition, none other than St. Paul consecrated a devout man named Prosperus first bishop of Tarragona. (This may be true, or it may have been fabricated to stimulate tourism.)

was *my* guest. "Anyway, when spring comes, when the work in Gaul is finished, I will be ready to visit some of the churches among the Jews in Syria, Cilicia, Galatia, over to Pisidian Antioch, Colossae, and Ephesus, then back through Lystra and Derbe. I should think he would wish to be by my side, by *our* side, for our return visit. He could steal some time with his mother! God willing it should take about a year. Well, anyway, please have him pray about it. Thanks." There were two significant features of Paul's message to Timothy. First, he didn't sound all that confident that the journey would actually take place. He seemed to me like he was convincing himself. Second, the fact he didn't mention it to Barnabas was telling. Come to think of it, there was a third: it is also telling that he assumed I would join him! Ha! I am *always* happy to serve.

We had good winds and fair weather all the way to Ostia. Before we disembarked, Paul gave to me his manuscript. It was entirely finished, he said, up to the benediction. He intended to put the finishing touches on that in his jail cell. I made arrangements with our friend, Theophilus, his chief jailer, to make sure, if something were to happen to Paul, that I would receive those final leaves, "and nobody else." Paul mentioned also that he could not stop thinking about Quintilian's view of the role of rhetoric in building bonds of community; how rhetoric "abides at the core of culture." "Luke, I know this is something about which you care very little, but please promise me you will always preserve, in the curriculum of our church schools, and in our program of study for preachers and teachers, the study of rhetoric and dialectic." Apparently, he had considered writing an exhortation to this effect, but felt he needed to stay focused on his letter, so he was trusting me. Time was short, he said. "Luke, you know how I have written so often about how the 'joints and ligaments' hold together the Body, in love?" "Absolutely, yes. Those are some of the most poignant images you employ." "Yes! And do you know why? Because, without strong bonds, the members cannot operate in harmony with one another; we would be all higgledy-piggledy. This in no way brings glory to Our Lord." "No. I understand." "Well," Paul tilted his head slightly and redoubled his intensity, "the more I think about what Quintilian said, the more I realize how vital is rhetoric in the formation of bonds of love. And dialectic and rhetoric go hand in hand to harmonize the ideas that steer our motion. Not to mention the benefits related to the right handling of God's Word, and of sermonizing! Our schools will neglect such wisdom at our peril." I think I understood what he was asking, but thought it best, under the circumstances to clarify details. Schoolmasters would require detailed instructions; strong schools were vital to our mission. "Any suggestions for specific works?" I asked. "Good question. Follow the pattern of the Hellenic Schools, generally. Liberal arts education is consistent, for the most part, with what we are about. It will certainly produce the kind of leaders we are after. Aristotle will be vital: his *Analytics, Topics* and *Rhetoric, Poetics,* and to some extent, his *Ethics,* but be careful with that one! That was the first work of Aristotle I started to question, the more I understood 'law and gospel.' Do you remember how concerned with his own works was Quintilian? That he did good, therefore he was good, in God's eyes?" "Yes," I said, "I must admit, I rolled my eyes a few times." "Straight out of Aristotle," Paul bobbed his head and gestured with his pointer finger, as though pointing at a specific scroll. "Plato has two especially good, very brief treatises: *The Gorgias* and *The Phaedrus.* Those are good. If that Quintilian ever writes anything on rhetoric or pedagogy, it would definitely be worth considering, too! Perhaps he will convert by th—. Say, we need to pray for that lad!" So we prayed that the Holy Spirit would draw Quintilian, and those around him, unto himself, and that he would find peace.

So, along with getting his manuscript published, I promised also to instruct our educators to teach rhetoric and dialectic as tools for building strong teachers and preachers, which would, in turn, build strong bonds that would help ensure the continued growth and sustenance of Christ's Body. I repeated it to him, more than once, to be sure I had his instructions correct. He was right, being a man of science, these were matters too esoteric and metaphysical for my temperament. But I did not allow ignorance of rhetoric and dialectic, nor of the business of publishing, to stop me from approaching these charges with a solemn sense of duty. They were the last wishes of a dying man. . . . A very important dying man.

Theophilus promised me I would have the final leaves. When they were delivered, to Lucina's, during the funeral, all was complete, up to and including the benediction. After the final "Amen," however, I found a few fragments of final greetings, as though he had been finishing up when they came for him. After everyone left, I stayed up late to complete the fragments. I was heartbroken to realize that, apparently, Paul still had hoped he would be released. Maybe he believed he'd outlive Nero? He wrote: "You should know that our brother Timothy has been released, with whom I shall see you if he comes soon." With tears in my eyes, I closed out the letter simply (and anonymously, per Paul's instructions,) "Greet all your leaders and all the saints. Greetings from Italy. Grace be with you all." I thought, "the less I add, the better." I confess to you, dear reader, that I added the final greetings and pray that you will not hold it against me. It seemed, under the circumstances, proper and salutary to conclude with a succinct, typical greeting. If I miscalculated, please forgive me.

16

Metanoia

30 YEARS LATER

"To whom will I dedicate this exercise in vanity??!! I have no one to whom I can now dedicate my efforts. O Cruel Fortune! I should have preceded my son in death; this is the proper order of things!" Quintilian pounded the table, palms open, to accentuate each individual lament. He sobbed and attempted to continue, but all that came out is, "My poor little Quintilian . . . " so he repeated that, convulsing.

"My little Quintilian" lived to age 10 and was beginning to show promise in the rhetorical arts. He was a natural born leader. He followed in death, by five years, both his mother and brother. Quintilian was alone. "O Deity that my grief worships . . . what am I to do? I would persevere for no interest of my own, and devote all my pains to the service of others, but I am tired. I cannot persevere. I cannot go on any longer! O God, I placed all my hopes in my little Quintilian. This work would have been such a blessing to the boy and he would have put its lessons to good use and he would be my legacy and he would have been a blessing to all the Empire and he would be comforted by these precepts from his father!" At this, the old man was again overcome with grief. He sobbed and thought of nothing; simply stared at the wall.

Gradually, it dawned on Quintilian that the Deity wished him to suffer for his sins. That he needed to try harder to forgive others and do good to them, that he had not tried hard enough. But he could scarcely entertain such a thought, for he knew in his heart, the one needful thing was *rest*. And so his inmost thoughts made a weak attempt at consolation;

from the wellsprings of memory bubbled to the surface something he had read on the road to Caesaraugusta, "Faith is the substance of things hoped for; the evidence of things not seen." He wasn't sure what it meant, but it seemed germane. Slowly, he exhales, so slowly at first glance one would have difficulty determining whether he breathed at all. Then the volume increased, intensified by the confluence of rage and anxiety behind it, to a primal scream: "Ahhhhhhhh! Why, God!!?? She was *so good*!!! So *innocent*!! I. Want. Her. Back!!! Why would you take her away from me?? The boys had their whole lives ahead of them!! That was cruel enough. *But my little dove* . . . ? Why, God?"! He was now sobbing again, beyond all restraint. "I want to see her!" he wailed, renouncing the one who robbed him of his love. "I want to see her again," he whimpered, miserably. "I want her . . . b-b-baaack," his head fell to the writing table with a self-mutilating thud. To knock himself out may have given momentary relief. He lay there for more than a little while. No thoughts formed. No emotion left to trouble and agitate him. "Owww!" Apparently the thud had done some good!

Abruptly, without warning, a palpably warm peace flooded his soul. "Faith is the substance of things hoped for; the evidence of things not seen." His meditation was brief, pointed, and effectual. He understood. He knew he could see her again. Paul, lo these many years ago, on the veranda, over olives, cheese, meat and wine, had said so. "Faith is the substance of things hoped for; the evidence of things not seen." He could see his little dove again. But he had to cross a divide. All his life he had served the Empire, and the gods of the Empire! He had made pledges; taken sacred oaths. How could he possibly, just to assuage this grief, how could he, Marcus Fabius Quintilianus, the renown legal counsel to Caesars, most highly regarded solicitor in all of Spain, public teacher of rhetorical arts, how could he buckle now to this weak-minded philosophy of rebels and cannibals? No. No, she was right. He was right. There is one God, and He is the father of us all. And Jesus was sent to show us the father. He came, how did he put it, "a High Priest forever, after the order of Melchoi . . . no, no Melchezidek." ." . . . and their belief was counted as righteousness. . . ." Paul had said something to the effect that, "all our good works wouldn't purchase a single drop of the blood that bought our salvation." It is so hard to . . . to stop. "Help me. . . . help me. . . . " Softly. Breathing; quivering. Deeply. He walked, without purpose, to the window, to stare off into the heavens, and breathe a little fresh air. There was, indeed, something most interesting at which to stare: A lone hawk, glided across the sky, off in the distance, near the foothills. This sight only intensified the quaking in his bosom. Quintilian, backed over to the desk, fell into the chair, more spent than he had ever been, or more at peace. He could not decide. It didn't matter.

After much time had passed, and nightfall was upon him, Quintilian gathered himself together, and looked around for a candle stand and towel to wipe his face and nose. He found a rag draped across a scroll, leaning against the pot where he had found the *Romans* scroll. He reached for the candle on the counter to his right, lit it, and took a look at the second scroll. He did not remember ever having noticed this one. When he read the title he gasped out loud. It was Paul's letter to the Hebrews! How in the world had that gotten here? He backed over to his work table, scroll in one hand and candle in the other, mindful to not drop either.

Puzzled as to how he had come by this treasure, this piece of hist—. What ho? A card fell from the scroll onto the table. Domatilla! "Dear Quintilian," the inscription read,

> I pray God washes away your worldly ambitions in the waters of Holy Baptism, that he gives you rest, and that you have ears to hear when the Spirit declares, "from dust you came and to dust you shall return." I commend my sons to your care and to the care of Almighty God. I hope to see you again when the political winds shift and I can return to Rome, to live out my days with my boys and their children and children's children.

Oh, sweet Domatilla, and sweet Flavius! I wish so that you would have been able to watch the boys grow! They were such good pupils. Such promise. But cruel fortune decided differently. Poor, poor Domatilla. I hope you found peace in your island prison. I hope Flavius found peace at last. I am so tired, he thought shaking his head at their misfortune. Maybe you were right, Domatilla. Maybe you were all right, my sweet dove, and Marcellus! Maybe you were all right!

Quintilian's soul ached so that he could not breathe. Looking for relief through those holy words, he poured over the manuscript, tears flowed freely. More than ten years since he had taken his bride home to meet the family in Hispania Tarraconensis. She had enjoyed it so much. Her girlish delight with the newfound joys of country living and of travel abroad was so endearing. She conceived Little Quintilian on that trip. "Her love was more precious to me than anything this world has to offer," Quintilian declared to himself. "She-She was my sweet little dove." And then he saw it.

In despair and desperation, he wiped his bloodshot eyes again and read these words:

> There remaineth therefore a rest to the people of God.
>
> For he that enters into his rest, has ceased from his own works, as God did from his.
>
> Let us strive therefore to enter into that rest. . . .

These words transported Quintilian to the veranda of Calagurritanum so quickly, with so much force, so vivid was the image of him talking with Paul, discussing this very passage, it physically took his breath away. "Strive to enter that rest." Ach! I was so proud then. So ambitious. So full of the world. What good has it done me? What good has it done? What good . . . ?" He gave up his meager, vain attempts to make sense of his quest for fame. So childish it was. His eyes instinctively moved down the scroll, but nothing registered. He was going through the motions of reading without actually allowing the meaning to penetrate, because he needed rest so acutely, he was no longer capable of meaning making. He could not conjure the energy to connect words, then grasp them, then translate them into coherent thought. He was *that* exhausted.

But then, the light from the candle on the table next to his wine goblet acted strangely. It bent and focused into a thin line that spanned the entire page, concentrating a preternatural light, blurred around the edges, on words, the meaning of which penetrated forcefully, though with no discernable effort on Quintilian's part. It was as though, having striven to the limit of his own abilities, his very mind and reason were suddenly being carried along, lighter than air, to a plane of understanding, of keen insight, beyond his own capacity. His spiritual eyes had been opened, and the fact that it was not his own doing was abundantly clear to him. He, not so much read, but felt these words:

> *Let us therefore come boldly unto the throne of grace, that we may obtain mercy, and find grace to help in time of need.*

Lord, I believe. I cannot see you, but I believe. Give me grace to believe. I want to believe, but I haven't the strength. Have mercy. Help me. . . . help me. . . . help me," he repeated this ostinato, softly, in an other-worldly cadence, both adagio and droning, originating deep within his breast, signaling the coda of Quintilian's restless soul. He slept.

Glossary

Caesaraugusta—modern day Zaragosa

chiasm—a poetic structure, especially prevalent in Hebrew and Greek composition, that utilizes an "insy/outsy" parallel structure as a means of
underscoring important points.

$$
\begin{array}{c}
A \\
\quad B \\
\qquad C \\
\qquad\quad D \\
\qquad C \\
\quad B \\
A
\end{array}
$$

(Note: in this example, "D" is, literally, the Point!)

"docere, delectare, movere"—The "Three Offices of Rhetoric"; "to teach, to
delight, and to persuade"

kairos—timing; important in both rhetoric and in joke-telling

Tarraco—modern day Tarragona

Calagurris—modern day Calahorra

Toletum—modern day Toledo

Burdigala—modern day Bourdeaux

Narbo—modern day Narbonne

dialectic—a test for the truth of propositions that are debatable, exemplified in the Socratic method; disputation (not to be confused with Hegelian Dialectic, which is significantly different

Hispania Terraconensis—one of three provinces in Roman Spain

elenchus—that point, in a dialectical competition, where the opponent either utters nonsense or contradicts himself. You win.

vir bonus—"good man"; central to Quintilian's definition of rhetoric, "the good man speaking well"

Index

Apollos 24, 26, 28–32, 124.

Aristotle "five intellectual virtues" 75, *Organon* 75 n 1, *Topica* discussed 85–86, dialectic and rhetoric counterparts of one another 95, follows the lead of Plato 114, ethos, pathos & logos 115.

Barnabas reports back to Paul in Ceasaraugusta 131–132.

Clement (eventual Bishop of Rome) "did not make the boat" 35, 66–69, off to Burdigala, 69, 125.

Domatilla wife of Flavius Clemens and first cousin to Emperor Domitian, who selected their two sons to be heirs to the throne and charged Quintilian with their education. Interestingly, George Alexander Kennedy observes that Flavius was executed for "atheism and Jewish practices"; she was banished to an island where the Christians there "claimed her as a convert." 138.

Elenchus 85.

kairos 106 n1.

Lucina's hospitality 7, 9, 23–24.

Luke eulogy on Paul 7–9, keen interest in *Celsus's Encyclopedia* 73, 101, engages in the "talky-talk" 109, styles apropos of homiletics versus persuasion 111, *vir bonus* 112–113, rhetoric and human excellence 114–115, considers composing a "witness" 120, the advent of catechesis 128, promises Paul to publish his letter to the Hebrews 133, resolves to honor Paul's request that parish schools always teach dialectic and rhetoric 135, finish Paul's final greeting, posthumously 135

Maximus (apprentice to Quintilian) 47, 123–124.

Melchizedek 19, 29–30, 77, 102, 105–106, 137.

Onesimus 124.

Paul, morning devotion 11–12, 33–35, teaching in Ostia 17–20, 22 (50 converts baptized in the Tiber River at Ostia), discusses his impending death with Lucina 24–25, and Apollos 24, 26, 28–32, Letter to the Hebrews 25, procession from Lucina's to the port 26, gruff with Onesimus 35, barks at Epaphras 38, *argumentum ex silentio* 38, discusses the gospel with Quintilian 59–61, discusses with Quintilian the word as written, spoken, and read 62, discusses with Quintilian virtue 71–72, suggests an extended dialectic on Truth, Beauty, and Goodness 73–74, discusses the Hellenic studies of his youth 79, discusses with Quintilian Aristotle's *Topica* 85–86, discusses with Quintilian the relation of dialectic to rhetoric; wisdom and eloquence, beauty to truth; pathos and style, how all these shape the soul 86–89, 94, 109, discusses with Quintilian the cultural role of rhetoric (see also, 89 n 1), story of his conversion 91, on Plato's *Phaedrus* 95, 114–115, shares the gospel with Quintilian 96–97, on the difference between preaching and persuading 97, 111, on rest 99–100, the "Let us" motif 101–104, decides to go to Oiasso rather than Brigantium 107–108, epiphany regarding the excellence of rhetoric 112–114, 116, "Love and Logos" 116, "Intellectual love of God" 116 (see also Richard M. Weaver), prays, with Luke, for Quintilian's salvation 117, returns from Oiasso to find Quintilian has left for Rome 120, big plans for Prosperus 129, "first fruits" of the missionary trip to Hispania 130, accuses Barnabas of making excuses 131, teaches Marcellus a primitive version of what will evolve into The Agnus Dei 127, impresses on Luke the importance of rhetorical studies to Christian students 133–134.

Pedagogy in Afer's school 55, 62, 103, with respect to catechesis (instruction in the faith) 127–128.

Probus (eventual husband of Xanthippe) 47, 124.

Prosperus (eventual Bishop of Tarragona 132 n 1,) 47, 124–125, declares his decision to enter full time ministry 132.

Quintilian 48, in court 49–51, discusses his pedigree in rhetorical studies (drawn directly from *Institutes of Oratory*) 53–55, 84, concerns over Jewish Revolt 55–56, discusses the gospel with Paul 59–61, discusses with Paul the word as written, spoken, and read 62, invites Paul to Calagurris 64, discusses with Paul virtue, 71–72, on *phronesis* versus *sophia* 73–74, holds forth on the beauty of well-ordered industry (drawn directly from *Institutes of Oratory*) 81–82, 84, discusses with Paul Aristotle's *Topica* 85–86, discusses with Paul the relation of dialectic to rhetoric; wisdom and eloquence, beauty to truth; pathos and style, how all these shape the soul 86–89, 94, 109, discusses with Paul the cultural role of rhetoric (see also, 89 n 1), on *vir bonus* 90, 112–113, on Plato's *Phaedrus* 95, 115, "ruminates" on the gospel 96–97, on the difference between preaching and persuading 97, 111, on rest 99–100, 102–104, 139, gets defensive 100–101, proposes to conclude the extended dialectic on Truth, Beauty, and Goodness 109, essence of his doctrine 114, epiphany regarding his need for rest and for peace 138–139.

Rhetoric and social bonds 82, 89, 112, end of 112, and politics 113, the capstone of the liberal arts 114, all about proper movement of the soul 114, hearts and minds 115, relevance to Christian's life together 133–134.

Simeon, Song of 41–42.

Team Alpha
    Apollos, Onesimus, and Timothy disembark in Narbo, follow the Via Aquitania through Southern Gaul, to Burdigala.

Team Beta
    Paul, Zenas, and Luke, follow Via Domitia from Tarraco to Caesaraugusta to Brigantium (at least, that was the plan).

Index

Team Gamma
> Barnabas, Aristarchus, and Epaphras moved along the coast, on the Via Herculea, from Tarraco to Valentia to Nova Carthago.

Timothy knows how to deal with Paul 37, keeps an eye on Apollos 38, 128,-129.

Xanthippe and Polyxene 41–45, 66–67, 124 n1, 125–126.

Zenas Paul's lawyer 13, 33, strong bonds of love with the young converts in Caesaraugusta 129.